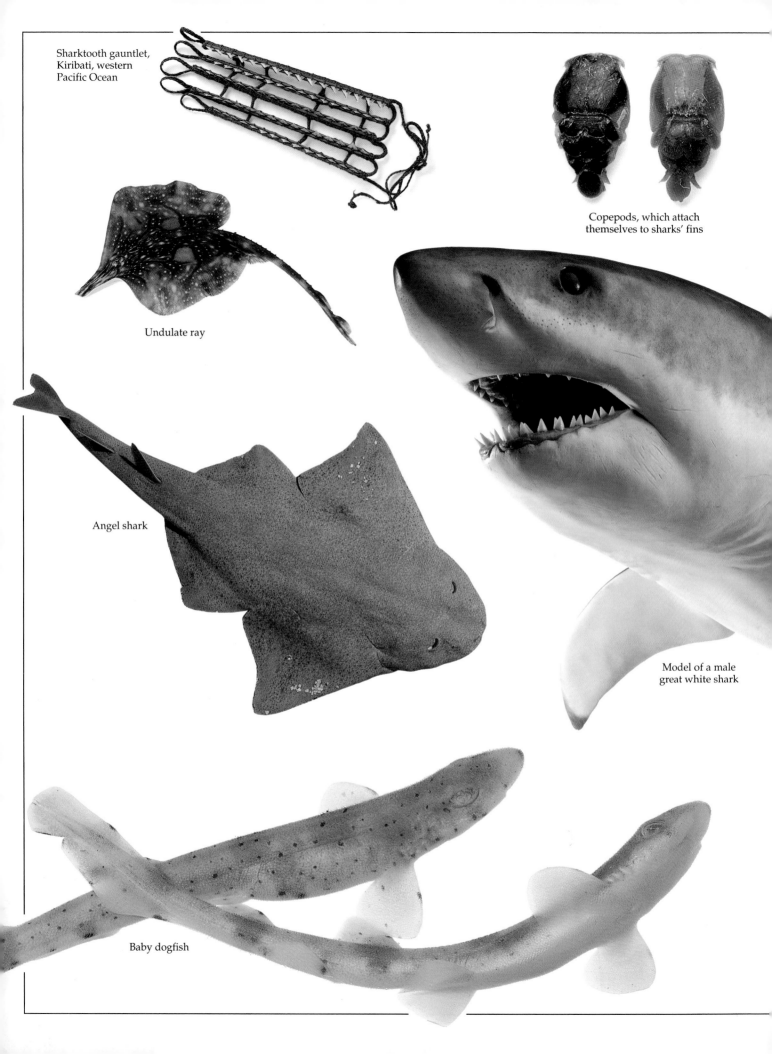

Sharktooth gauntlet, Kiribati, western Pacific Ocean

Copepods, which attach themselves to sharks' fins

Undulate ray

Angel shark

Model of a male great white shark

Baby dogfish

Sharktooth "brass" knuckles from the Hawaiian Islands

EYEWITNESS BOOKS

SHARK

Fossil tooth of a megalodon

Written by
MIRANDA MACQUITTY

Epaulette shark

Shark-shaped gold weight, from Ghana, West Africa

Sharktooth necklace from New Zealand

Swell shark

ALFRED A. KNOPF • NEW YORK

Port
Jackson
shark

Pair of starry
smoothhounds

A DORLING KINDERSLEY BOOK

Leopard shark

Fossil of
Ptychodus
tooth

Project editor Marion Dent
Art editor Jill Plank
Managing editor Helen Parker
Managing art editor Julia Harris
Production Louise Barratt
Picture research Suzanne Williams
Special photography Frank Greenaway, Dave King
Editorial consultant Dr. Geoffrey Waller
Model makers Graham High, Jeremy Hunt
Special thanks Sea Life Centres (UK)

Long spear for
catching sharks,
Nicobar Islands, India

Rayskin-
covered
scabbard used
by Ashanti
tribe, Ghana,
West Africa

This is a Borzoi Book published by
Alfred A. Knopf, Inc.

This Eyewitness Book has been conceived by
Dorling Kindersley Limited and Editions Gallimard

First American edition, 1992

Shark rattle,
Samoa, South
Pacific

Manufactured in Singapore
0 9

Library of Congress Cataloging-in-Publication Data
MacQuitty, Miranda.
Shark / by Miranda MacQuitty :
[special photography by Frank Greenaway, Dave King].
—1st American ed.
p. cm. — (Eyewitness Books)
"A Dorling Kindersley book" —T.p.
Includes index.
Summary: Describes, in text and photographs, the
physical characteristics, behavior, and life cycle of
various types of sharks.
1. Sharks—Juvenile literature. [1.Sharks.]
I. Greenaway, Frank, ill. II. King, Dave, ill. III. Title.
QL638.9.M25 1992 597' .31—dc20 92-4712
ISBN 0-679-81683-6
ISBN 0-679-91683-0 (lib. bdg.)

Color reproduction by Colourscan, Singapore
Printed in Singapore by Toppan

Contents

Model of a
great white
shark

What is a shark?

MANY PEOPLE THINK of sharks as mean and menacing, with their pointed snouts, fearsome teeth, and staring eyes. Sharks are skillful predators, but only a few are a danger to people. The 375 or so species of shark range in size from the dwarf dogshark at about 6.5 in (16 cm) long to the whale shark at over 40 ft (12 m) long, but half the species are less than 3.3 ft (1 m) long. Not all sharks are as streamlined as this spinner shark. Angel sharks have flat bodies; horn sharks are blunt-headed; and bamboo sharks are long and flexible. All sharks belong to one class of fish called Chondrichthyes, which have skeletons made of gristlelike cartilage. Sharks live in the sea, though a few live in or swim into inland waters.

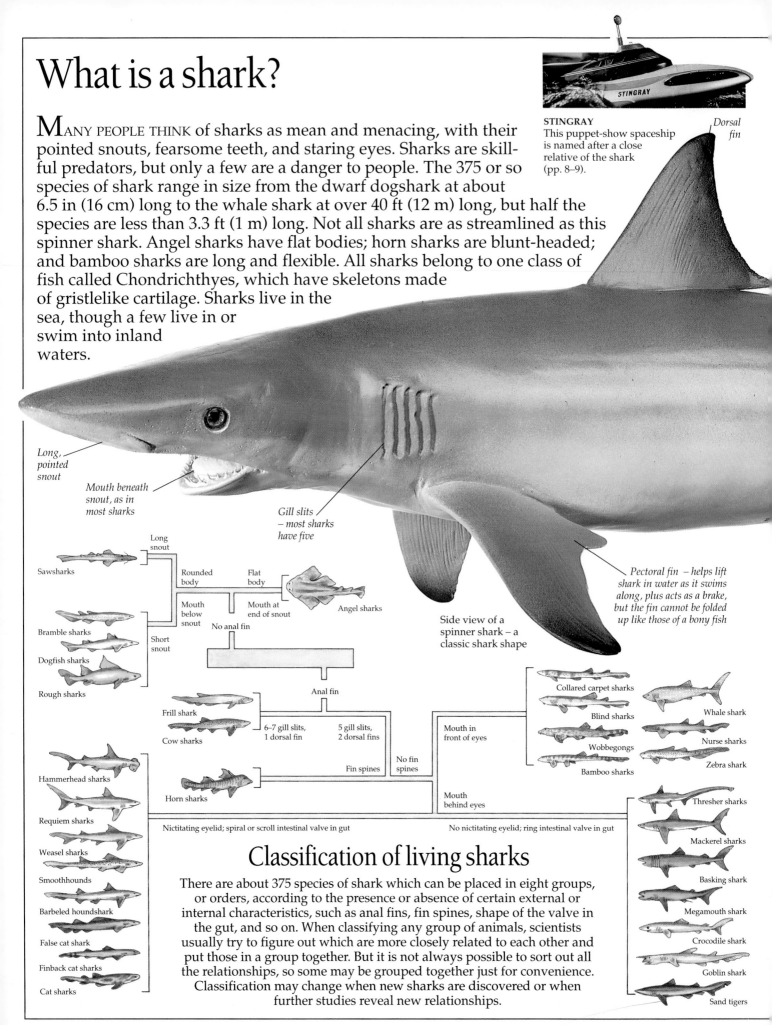

STINGRAY
This puppet-show spaceship is named after a close relative of the shark (pp. 8–9).

Dorsal fin

Long, pointed snout

Mouth beneath snout, as in most sharks

Gill slits – most sharks have five

Pectoral fin – helps lift shark in water as it swims along, plus acts as a brake, but the fin cannot be folded up like those of a bony fish

Side view of a spinner shark – a classic shark shape

Sawsharks

Long snout

Rounded body

Flat body

Mouth below snout

Mouth at end of snout

Angel sharks

Bramble sharks

Dogfish sharks

Short snout

No anal fin

Rough sharks

Frill shark

Cow sharks

6–7 gill slits, 1 dorsal fin

5 gill slits, 2 dorsal fins

Anal fin

Mouth in front of eyes

Collared carpet sharks

Blind sharks

Wobbegongs

Bamboo sharks

Whale shark

Nurse sharks

Zebra shark

Hammerhead sharks

Horn sharks

Fin spines

No fin spines

Mouth behind eyes

Requiem sharks

Weasel sharks

Nictitating eyelid; spiral or scroll intestinal valve in gut

No nictitating eyelid; ring intestinal valve in gut

Thresher sharks

Mackerel sharks

Smoothhounds

Barbeled houndshark

Classification of living sharks

There are about 375 species of shark which can be placed in eight groups, or orders, according to the presence or absence of certain external or internal characteristics, such as anal fins, fin spines, shape of the valve in the gut, and so on. When classifying any group of animals, scientists usually try to figure out which are more closely related to each other and put those in a group together. But it is not always possible to sort out all the relationships, so some may be grouped together just for convenience. Classification may change when new sharks are discovered or when further studies reveal new relationships.

Basking shark

False cat shark

Megamouth shark

Crocodile shark

Finback cat sharks

Goblin shark

Cat sharks

Sand tigers

THOUSANDS OF TEETH
Sharks never run out of teeth.
When the front ones become
worn or break, they are replaced by new ones in the row
behind (right). Some sharks
shed one or two teeth at a time,
while others, like spiny dogfish
and cookiecutters (pp. 44–45),
replace a whole row at a time.
As the shark grows, its new
teeth are larger than the ones
replaced. During its life, a shark
will produce thousands of teeth.
Each new tooth forms in the
shark's gums and rotates forward
until it eventually drops out. Sharks'
teeth are embedded in their gums
and are not directly attached to their
jaws, like those of bony fish.

Jaws and teeth
of sand
tiger
shark

Skin of
bramble
shark

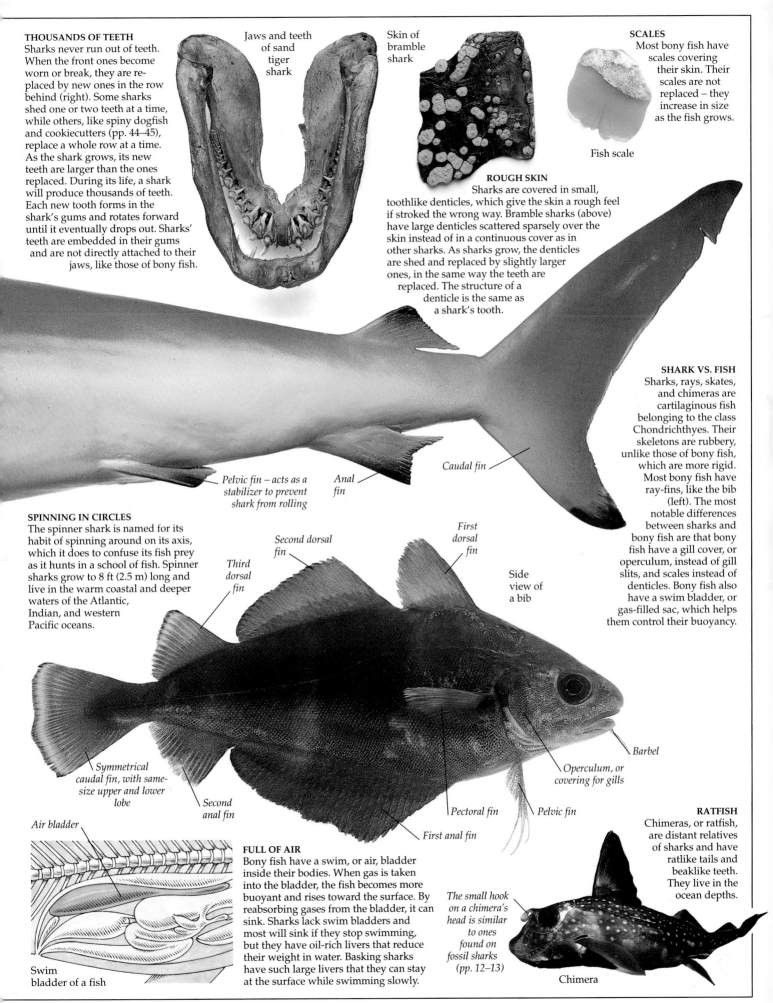

SCALES
Most bony fish have
scales covering
their skin. Their
scales are not
replaced – they
increase in size
as the fish grows.

Fish scale

ROUGH SKIN
Sharks are covered in small,
toothlike denticles, which give the skin a rough feel
if stroked the wrong way. Bramble sharks (above)
have large denticles scattered sparsely over the
skin instead of in a continuous cover as in
other sharks. As sharks grow, the denticles
are shed and replaced by slightly larger
ones, in the same way the teeth are
replaced. The structure of a
denticle is the same as
a shark's tooth.

SHARK VS. FISH
Sharks, rays, skates,
and chimeras are
cartilaginous fish
belonging to the class
Chondrichthyes. Their
skeletons are rubbery,
unlike those of bony fish,
which are more rigid.
Most bony fish have
ray-fins, like the bib
(left). The most
notable differences
between sharks and
bony fish are that bony
fish have a gill cover, or
operculum, instead of gill
slits, and scales instead of
denticles. Bony fish also
have a swim bladder, or
gas-filled sac, which helps
them control their buoyancy.

*Pelvic fin – acts as a
stabilizer to prevent
shark from rolling*

*Anal
fin*

Caudal fin

SPINNING IN CIRCLES
The spinner shark is named for its
habit of spinning around on its axis,
which it does to confuse its fish prey
as it hunts in a school of fish. Spinner
sharks grow to 8 ft (2.5 m) long and
live in the warm coastal and deeper
waters of the Atlantic,
Indian, and western
Pacific oceans.

*Second dorsal
fin*

*First
dorsal
fin*

*Third
dorsal
fin*

Side
view of
a bib

*Symmetrical
caudal fin, with same-
size upper and lower
lobe*

*Second
anal fin*

Barbel

*Operculum, or
covering for gills*

Air bladder

FULL OF AIR
Bony fish have a swim, or air, bladder
inside their bodies. When gas is taken
into the bladder, the fish becomes more
buoyant and rises toward the surface. By
reabsorbing gases from the bladder, it can
sink. Sharks lack swim bladders and
most will sink if they stop swimming,
but they have oil-rich livers that reduce
their weight in water. Basking sharks
have such large livers that they can stay
at the surface while swimming slowly.

Pectoral fin

Pelvic fin

First anal fin

Swim
bladder of a fish

*The small hook
on a chimera's
head is similar
to ones
found on
fossil sharks
(pp. 12–13)*

RATFISH
Chimeras, or ratfish,
are distant relatives
of sharks and have
ratlike tails and
beaklike teeth.
They live in the
ocean depths.

Chimera

Close relatives

THE MIGHTY MANTA
Manta rays, or devilfish, have enormous
pectoral fins (wings) that measure up to 23 ft
(7 m) across. This magnificent female specimen,
caught off the New Jersey coast, weighed almost
2,860 lb (1,300 kg). These harmless filter feeders
use the large lobes on their heads to channel
plankton into their wide mouths.

A GRACEFUL MANTA RAY SWIMMING ALONG with slow beats of its
huge wings looks nothing like a sleek reef shark. Yet rays and
their cousins – skates, guitarfish, and sawfish – all belong to
the same group as sharks, called elasmobranchs. Members of
this group have cartilaginous skeletons, which are flexible like
rubber, and gill slits instead of the flaplike opercula, or gill
covers, found in bony fish and chimeras (pp. 6–7). All rays
have winglike pectoral fins running the length of the head and
body, and gill slits on their undersides. Most rays live on the
seabed, where they feed on fish,
shellfish, and worms.

Starry ray

*Spines increase in size along
body from minute at snout to
larger at tip of tail*

Blonde ray

Spotted ray

**SPOT THE
DIFFERENCE**
There is a great
variety among
rays in the pattern
on their upper side.
The pattern helps to
camouflage them while
they rest on the seabed.
The spots on the blonde
ray go right to the edge of
its pectoral fins; those on the
spotted ray do not. The undersides of rays are usually white.

*Second
dorsal fin*

First dorsal fin

Painted ray

Guitarfish

*Spines along
back for extra
protection
against
predators*

RAY OR SKATE?
Thornback ray is often sold
as edible skate, but common
skate actually grows to twice
the thornback's size, reaching
6.5 ft (2 m) long.

STRANGE RAYS
Guitarfish (50 species) and sawfish (six species) belong
to the same group as rays. Guitarfish live mostly in
warmer seas, but sawfish are also found in rivers and lakes.
Sawfish look like sawsharks but do not have the two long
barbels in the middle of their "saws," and their gill slits are on
the undersides of their bodies, not on the sides of their heads. Sawfish and sawsharks use their saws for feeding and defending themselves.

Sawfish

BABY RAY
This one-month-
old spotted
baby ray will
take eight
years before
it matures
and is able
to reproduce.

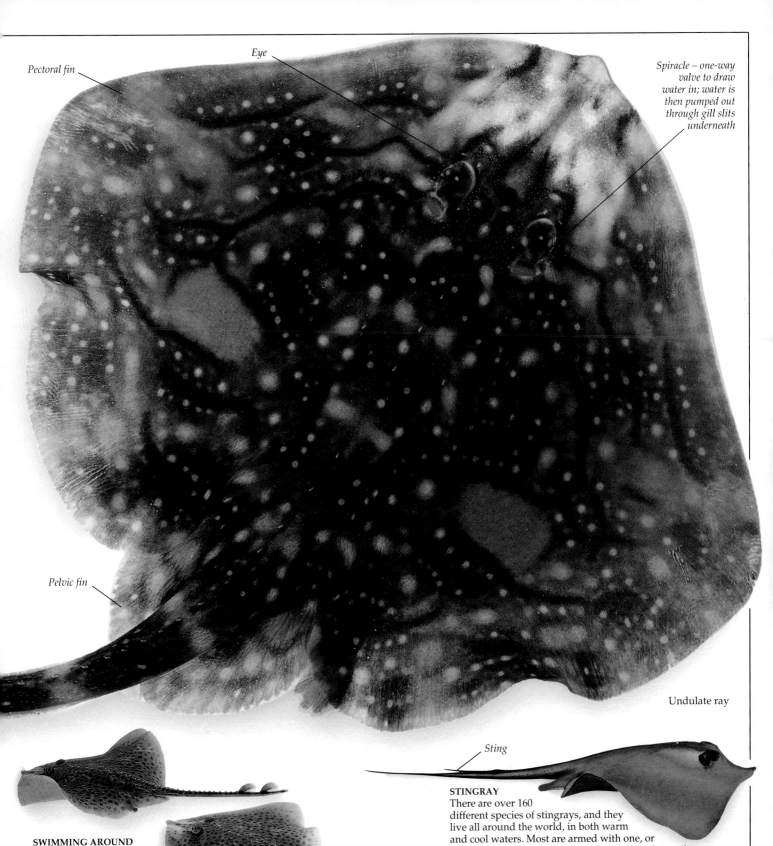

Eye

Pectoral fin

Spiracle – one-way valve to draw water in; water is then pumped out through gill slits underneath

Pelvic fin

Undulate ray

Sting

STINGRAY
There are over 160 different species of stingrays, and they live all around the world, in both warm and cool waters. Most are armed with one, or sometimes several, venomous spines on their tails.

SWIMMING AROUND
Most rays swim by using their pectoral fins. But electric rays, sawfish, and some species of guitarfish swim in the same way as sharks do, by sculling with their tails. This spotted ray's tail is too spindly to provide much propulsion, so undulations, or waves, pass down the length of the ray's pectoral fins from front to back. As rays swim along, they appear to fly through the water. The up-and-down motion of the pectoral fins, or wings, is shown much better in species with enormous wings, like the manta ray. These giant rays are even able to leap clear out of the water, sometimes up to 5 ft (1.5 m).

Typical swimming sequence of rays

Inside a shark

Packaged neatly inside this spinner shark's body are all the organs that keep it alive. To breathe, sharks have gills that absorb oxygen from the water and release carbon dioxide back into it. These gases are transported to and from the gills by the blood. The heart pumps the blood around the body, delivering oxygen and nutrients while taking away carbon dioxide and other wastes. To get energy for all their activities, including growth and repair, sharks need to eat. Food passes from the mouth into the digestive system, which is like a large tube. From the mouth the food goes down the gullet into the stomach, where digestion begins, and then into the intestine where digested food is absorbed. Indigestible wastes collect in the rectum to be passed out of the body. Digested food is further processed in the large liver. Kidneys remove wastes from the blood and regulate blood concentration. Large muscles in the body wall keep the shark swimming, and the skeleton and skin provide support. The brain coordinates the shark's actions with signals or instructions passed back and forth along the spinal cord. Finally, sharks, like all animals, cannot live forever and must reproduce to carry on the species. Female sharks have ovaries that produce eggs, and males produce sperm from their testes. When sperm meets egg, a new life begins.

DANGER BELOW
Sharks have been known to attack people coming down into water, as this Australian parachutist will soon discover.

Paired kidneys regulate waste products to keep the concentration of body fluids just above that of seawater, or sharks will dehydrate

Segmented swimming muscles contract alternately, sending a wave motion from head to tail

Model of female spinner shark, showing internal anatomy

Vent between claspers for disposing of body wastes

Clasper (male reproductive organ)

Male shark

Female shark (claspers absent)

Cloaca (opening for reproduction, and vent for waste disposal)

MALE OR FEMALE
All male sharks have a pair of claspers that are formed from the inner edge of their pelvic fins. During mating, one of the claspers is rotated forward and inserted into the female's body opening, or cloaca. Sperm is pumped down a groove in the clasper into the female, so fertilization of her eggs takes place inside her body.

Rectal gland (third kidney) passes excess salt out of the body through the vent

Scroll valve in intestine, or gut; some sharks have spiral or ring valves

Left lobe of large liver

Caudal fin

ALL IN THE TAIL
Sharks have a vertebral column, or backbone, that extends into the upper lobe of their caudal fin, or tail. This type of caudal fin is called a heterocercal tail, as opposed to those in most bony fish, where the upper lobe does not contain an extension of the upper vertebral column. Cartilaginous rods and dermal filaments help to strengthen the shark's tail.

Vertebral column

Cartilaginous rod

Dermal filament

BRAIN POWER
Some sharks have brains that are similar in weight to those of birds and mammals, when compared to their overall body weight. The olfactory bulb, or sensory part of the nose, is close to the front part of the brain.

Olfactory bulb, or nasal sac

Forebrain

Midbrain

Hindbrain

Brain of a lemon shark

Ovary (eggs visible within its wall). When ripe, eggs pass into a tube for fertilization

Gill arch with gill filaments, where respiration takes place

Cartilage support of gill arch, forming a hoop around the gullet

Jaw-opening muscle pulls jaws forward so teeth protrude

Nostril

Tongue is rigid, supported by a pad of cartilage

Jaw-closing muscle

Cartilage in floor of gullet

Aorta, with branchial arteries

Heart

Open gill slits (below)

Closed gill slits (below)

BLOOD CIRCULATION
Blood from the body collects in the first chamber of the shark's heart; it is then pumped through the second and third; the fourth prevents blood from flowing back into the heart. The aorta and branchial arteries circulate blood to the gills, where each branchial artery divides into tiny blood vessels in the gill filaments. As seawater passes over the gills, oxygen is picked up and carbon dioxide released.

Cartilage at base of pectoral fin

Cartilage of pectoral girdle supports pectoral fins and protects heart

Gall bladder

Pectoral fin

FOOD PROCESSOR
Food begins its digestion process in the shark's stomach, then passes into the intestine, where the multi-layered scroll valve increases the area that absorbs digested food. A greenish-yellow fluid, stored in the gallbladder, is released into the gut, where it helps fats be absorbed. The shark's large liver also aids in digestion and in processing fats, carbohydrates, and proteins.

First dorsal fin

Stomach's descending limb

OPEN, SHUT
As the shark breathes, water comes in through its mouth, passes over the gills, and out the gill slits. A nurse shark pumps water across its gills by closing its mouth and contracting the mouth and gullet walls. When the mouth opens, the gill slits shut; when the mouth closes, the gill slits open.

Second dorsal fin

Anal fin

Rear view of whole body of shark, showing gullet

Pelvic fin

Stomach's ascending limb

Spleen produces red blood cells

Pancreas produces enzymes to help digest food in gut

11

Ancient sharks

THE FIRST SHARKS appeared in the ancient seas 400 million years ago, about 200 million years before dinosaurs roamed the earth. At that time there were no reptiles, birds, or mammals. The remains of some of these early sharks were fossilized when they sank to the bottom of the sea and became covered with layers of sand and other sediment. Hard parts, like spines and teeth, fossilized more readily than soft parts, which often rotted away. Sometimes all that is left are impressions of the sharks in rocks. Fossil shark teeth are common because these ancient sharks, like their living descendants, shed many teeth in a lifetime. Sharks' rubbery skeletons, made of cartilage, were preserved less often than the hard skeletons of bony fish. Shark fossils are often discovered in rocks on land that, in prehistoric times, was under the sea. Scientists can tell how old fossils are from the age of the rocks in which they are found. The earliest groups of sharks became extinct, but the descendants of some groups that first appeared about 200 million years ago – like the bullheads (pp. 40–41), cat sharks, and cow sharks – are alive today.

A megalodon's tooth (actual size)

Serrated (notched) edge for cutting

Actual-size tooth of a great white shark (pp. 28–31)

Flat, ridged side for crushing prey

Tooth of *Ptychodus*

WHAT BIG TEETH!
Shown above is a fossil tooth of a megalodon ("big tooth"), compared to one from its living relative, the great white shark. Megalodons reached 43 ft (13 m) long and must have been fearsome predators when they cruised the seas about 15 million years ago. A megalodon probably used its teeth for slashing deep into large prey, as great whites do today. The small, ridged tooth is from *Ptychodus* from 120 million years ago. These sharks probably ate shellfish, crushing them against their hard tooth ridges. They died out at the same time as the dinosaurs, about 65 million years ago.

JUST A JUVENILE
Looking much the same as its living relative – the lesser spotted dogfish (pp. 20–21) – this young shark died at least 65 million years ago. It is preserved in a piece of rock from Lebanon, in the Middle East.

Caudal fin like a mako's – upper lobe strengthened by extended vertebral column, like all sharks

Second dorsal fin would have had a short spine in front

Relatively small dorsal fin, also had a spine in front

CLADOSELACHE
This model reveals what *Cladoselache*, one of the earliest known sharks, probably looked like. Almost 6.6 ft (2 m) long, this shark swam in the ancient seas about 360 million years ago. It had a powerful tail, like a mako shark (pp. 16–17), so it could probably swim fast, but the pectoral fins were broader than those of fast, modern sharks, possibly making it a less agile swimmer. *Cladoselache* could swim well enough to catch fish, some of which have even been preserved in the stomachs of fossils. Unlike the mouths of many modern sharks, *Cladoselache's* was at the tip of its snout.

Small, broad-based, triangular pelvic fin in this model projects horizontally

Caudal fin

Dorsal spine

Spine on second dorsal fin

Hook on head for holding female during mating

Pectoral fin

Anal fin

Fossil of *Hybodus*

Pelvic fin

HYBODUS
Relatives of this kind of shark appeared about 320 million years ago and died out about 65 million years ago, along with the dinosaurs. *Hybodus* appeared about 240 million years ago and grew to about 8 ft (2.5 m) long. Males had claspers attached to their pelvic fins, as well as one or two hooks on their heads to hold onto females during mating. *Hybodus* also had an anal fin like some modern sharks.

Back brush

Head pad

BRUSH CUT
Stethacanthus, at 3.3 ft (1 m) long, was a strange-looking shark with a big brush of denticles on its back and a pad of denticles on its head. Those on the brush pointed forward, and the ones on the head pointed backward. If the shark bent back its head, it may have been able to grip larger fish. Also, the two sets of denticles, when opposing each other, could look like a big mouth and frighten off attackers. Whatever preyed on *Stethacanthus*, which lived over 300 million years ago, got a prickly mouthful.

GREAT WHITE JAWS
One of the largest sets of great white jaws in the world is 22.5 in (57.5 cm) wide.

FIN AND HEAD SPINES
Some ancient sharks had spines (left) in front of their dorsal fins, which may have protected them against large predators. Males of some early sharks had one or two hooks (right) on their heads for holding onto females while mating. Male chimeras still have hooks on their heads (pp. 6–7).

Fin spine

Head spine

Victorian boy, 40 in (102 cm) tall

Large, round eye

GIANT JAWS OF A MEGALODON
A reconstruction of the jaws of a megalodon is shown above, with the jaws of its living relative – the great white – inside them to the same scale. There has been much speculation as to the size of a megalodon's jaws. Although an early estimate put them at 9 ft (2.7 m) across, more recent discoveries prove that a megalodon's jaws measured less than 6 ft (1.8 m) across, as shown in this latest reconstruction from the Smithsonian Institution in Washington, D.C. Megalodons' ancestors appeared about 60 million years ago, and they themselves still existed until about 12,000 years ago. Our ancestors may have seen these monstrous sharks.

Triangular, broad-based pectoral fin

This model of Cladoselache has seven gill slits, but it is now known to have had only five

Mouth at end of snout, rather than on underside

Amazing grace

SHARKS ARE GRACEFUL swimmers. They propel themselves through the water by beating their tails from side to side. The pectoral fins are held out from the body, and as water flows over them, lift is generated to keep the shark from sinking. Further lift is produced by the upper lobe of the tail, which tends to push the head down, so that the shark can swim level. Shark fins are not nearly as flexible as those of bony fish, but small changes to the angle at which the fins are held control whether the shark goes up, down, left, or right. Pectoral fins are also used for braking. Some sharks that live on the seabed, such as horn sharks (pp. 40–41) and epaulette sharks, can use their pectoral fins to crawl along the bottom. Unlike bony fish, sharks cannot move their pectoral fins like paddles so are unable to swim backward or hover in the water. They also lack a swim bladder, which acts as a buoyancy aid in bony fish. However, sharks do have an oil-rich liver (pp. 10–11), which helps reduce their weight in water.

THE THREE GRACES
According to Greek mythology, these three daughters of Zeus were the goddesses of grace and beauty.

TAIL END
Undulations, or S-shaped waves, pass down a shark's body as it moves forward (above). The tail bends more than the rest of the body, producing a forward thrust.

STARRY SMOOTHHOUND
The denticles on a shark's skin align in the direction of travel, helping to reduce drag. These denticles may trap a film of water, which would help sharks move more easily through the water.

CRUISING
With pectoral fins held straight out from its sides, the starry smoothhound (right) keeps swimming at the same level. The two dorsal fins keep the shark from rolling, and its tail gives a forward thrust.

14

One-year-old
leopard shark,
15 in (38 cm) long

SEE HOW IT BENDS
Leopard sharks (above) have flexible
bodies, so they can turn around
in small spaces. Like their close
relatives, the smoothhounds, leopard
sharks spend much of their time cruising
close to the bottom and also resting on the seabed.

A LITTLE LIFT GOES A LONG WAY
The large pectoral fins of the starry smoothhound (left) are similar
to an airplane's wings, because they provide lift to keep the shark from
sinking. When tilted they can also act as brakes, like the flaps on the
wings of an airplane, which are raised on landing. Submarines have
horizontal fins, called hydrofoils, which lift them upward like those
of a shark. Just like a hydrofoil, the leading (or front) edge of a shark's
pectoral fin is rounded and the trailing (or rear) edge is thin, so water
flows over it more easily. The pointed snout and tapered body are
streamlined and give little resistance to the water.

FULL STEAM AHEAD
A great white shark
(above) usually cruises
at about 1.8 mph
(3 kph). Its bulky body
hardly moves at all,
while its tail beats from
side to side. When
closing in on a kill, the
great white puts on an
impressive burst of
speed of up to 15 mph
(25 kph).

BIG SURPRISE!
Great whites can bend
their bodies but are
not nearly as flexible
as smaller sharks.
They have to surprise
their prey rather than
out-maneuver them.

15

Continued on next page

Tails and more tails

The shape of a shark's tail suits its way of life. Many sharks have tail fins with an upper lobe that is larger than the lower; as the tail swings from side to side, this larger lobe produces lift, which tends to push the head down. This is compensated for by lift from the pectoral fins, which keeps the shark from sinking to the bottom. In fast sharks, like the mako and great white, these two lobes are almost equal in size. Lift may also come from the base of the tail, which in the mako has small, horizontal keels (ridges). The extra height of these more symmetrically shaped tails gives a more powerful thrust. Slow bottom-dwellers, like the nurse shark, have less powerful tails, and their swimming motion is more eel-like, with obvious waves passing down to their tails.

BONNETHEAD'S TAIL
Bonnetheads are small hammer-heads (pp. 42–43), which grow to about 5 ft (1.5 m) in length. Like all sharks', the bonnethead's tail's upper lobe contains an extension of the vertebral column and is usually larger than the lower lobe. The upper lobe is at an angle and is above the shark's midline (imagine a line drawn through the shark from the tip of its snout to the end of its body).

Tail of a bonnethead shark

THRESHER'S TAIL
The upper lobe of the tail of a thresher shark (left) is as long as its body. From 5–8 ft (1.5–2.5 m) in length, the tails of the three different types of thresher (pp. 58–59) are by far the longest of any shark. A thresher uses its tail to stun its prey. It can also inflict nasty injuries on anglers when the sharks are hauled on board.

Tail of a thresher shark

Keel

GREAT WHITE'S TAIL
The upper and lower lobes of a great white's tail fin are almost equal in size. They lie high above, and low below, the shark's midline respectively. The keel helps the big shark to turn. The first dorsal fin is rigid and prevents the shark from rolling. Also, a great white can jump out of the water.

Tail view of a model of a great white shark (pp. 28–29)

HEAVENLY TAKEOFF
To lift its huge body off the seabed, the angel shark beats its tail back and forth while tipping its large pectoral and pelvic fins for maximum lift. Once off the seabed, angels propel themselves forward by sculling with their tails, but they do not undulate, or wave, their pectoral fins like rays.

MIDAIR MAKO
Makos (pp. 26–27) are probably the fastest sharks in the sea, reaching speeds estimated to be 20 mph (32 kph) for a few moments. When caught on an angler's line, they leap clear of the surface in an effort to escape (above). Their tails are the same shape as another fast fish, the tuna, and like tunas they have keels along the base of their tails, which may give them more maneuverability, and perhaps provide some lift. They are active predators, pursuing mainly fish.

Lower lobe of angel shark's tail fin (pp. 36–37) is longer than upper lobe

SWELL TAIL
Smaller than nurse sharks, at 3.3 ft (1 m) long, swell sharks (right) are sluggish animals, spending the day resting on the seabed and at night swimming close to the bottom. Their tails are set barely above their midlines.

HORN SHARK'S TAIL
The lower lobe of the horn shark's tail (pp. 40–41) is more developed than the swell shark's. The tail of this 3.3-ft (1-m) shark is also at a low angle to its midline, and it is a slow swimmer.

TAIL OF A NURSE SHARK
Nurse sharks, at 10 ft (3 m) long, are rather slow swimmers and use their tails (right) for cruising near the bottom.

Blue shark's
nictitating
eyelid

Pore

Making sense

SHARKS HAVE THE SAME FIVE SENSES as people – they can see, hear, smell, taste, and touch. There is also a sixth sense that allows sharks to detect weak electrical signals generated by their prey. This electro-sense may also help them to navigate on their journeys in the sea. The underwater world is very different from our own. Light levels decrease with depth, and colors fade to blues. Sound travels five times faster and farther. Odors are dissolved in water, not wafted in the air. Sharks can detect vibrations made by animals moving through the water, giving them the sense called "distant touch." It is hard to find out exactly how a shark perceives its world, but studies on their behavior and how sense organs work give some idea about what it is like to be a shark.

Nostril

METAL DETECTOR
Sweeping a metal detector back and forth to find buried metal objects is like the way hammerheads (pp. 42–43) hunt for fish hiding in the sand.

GOING TO ITS HEAD
Like us, a shark's major sense organs are on its head. Seen on this blue shark are the eye, nostril, and sensory pores, which detect weak electrical signals. The eye is partly covered by a third eyelid, called a nictitating (or blinking) eyelid; it protects the eye when the shark attacks prey or nears unfamiliar objects. As the shark swims along, water flows through the nostril beneath the tip of the snout, bringing a constant stream of odors.

FEEDING FRENZY
When sharks are feeding on bait, they may become overexcited and snap wildly at their food. They may bite each other and even tear one another apart.

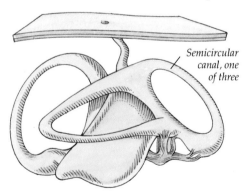

Semicircular canal, one of three

THE INNER EAR
Sharks do not have external ear flaps, but have ears inside their heads on either side of the brain case. Three semicircular canals placed at right angles to each other are like those found in the ears of all vertebrates. These canals help a shark figure out which way it has turned in the water. Receptors in the inner ear, like those in the lateral line on the skin, pick up sounds traveling through the water. Each ear has a small duct which leads to a pore on the top of the shark's head.

Epaulette's slit-shaped pupil

Dogfish with closed pupil

Angel shark's pupil

Reef shark with vertical pupil

Horn shark's pupil

Ray with light-blocking screen

ALL KINDS OF EYES
According to how much light there is, the iris in a shark's eyes contracts or expands to alter the size of the pupil. The tapetum lucidum, a layer of cells at the back of the eye, reflects light back onto the retina, where images are focused, making maximum use of any available light. This helps sharks to see in dim light. Cats also have a tapetum, which is why their eyes reflect lights shined at them. On bright, sunny days a shark can shield its tapetum with a layer of pigment. Like a human retina, a shark retina has two types of cells – rods work in dim light and are sensitive to light changes; cones resolve details and probably allow sharks to see in color.

DISTANT TOUCH
Sharks have a lateral-line system running down each side of the body and onto the head. The lines are small canals with tiny pores beneath which are cells with minute hairs. Scattered over the body are similar hair cells called pit organs, which like the lateral lines pick up vibrations.

Lateral line

Starry smoothhound showing lateral line

EYES ON STALKS
Hammerheads' eyes are on the end of their head projections, giving them a good view as they swing their heads back and forth. The nostrils are widely spaced on the front of the head, helping them detect where an odor is coming from. The head projections are packed with ampullae of Lorenzini, which detect electrical signals from hidden fish.

Compass

Imaginary magnet

North-south axis

Earth's magnetic field

COMPASS SENSE
Some sharks migrate hundreds of miles and seem to know where they are going, in what to us is a featureless ocean. Scientists think sharks have compass sense to guide them. In a real compass, a magnetic needle swings around to align itself to the earth's magnetic field. The earth's magnetic field (above) is created by its core, which acts like a giant magnet. Sharks seem able to swim in one direction by sensing changes in their own electrical fields in relation to the earth's magnetic field. Corrections have to be made for speed and direction of ocean currents, which may sweep the shark off course. Sharks may also be able to navigate by detecting magnetic patterns on the seabed.

DUCKBILLED PLATYPUS
One of the few animals, apart from sharks, that has a sixth sense enabling it to detect electrical signals of its prey, is the duckbilled platypus from Australia. The platypus's electro-receptors are on the left-hand side of its bill. Platypuses live in streams, where they hunt for insects and other small creatures on the river bottom.

Nurse shark

Barbel

FEELERS AND TASTE BUMPS
The pair of barbels, or feelers, on the nurse shark's nose (right) means it can feel prey such as shrimp hiding in the sand. Many of the sharks that live on the seabed have barbels, which they use to probe the sand for food. Barbels may also play a role in taste. Sharks have taste buds on bumps in their mouths and gullets (left). They will spit out something, if they do not like its taste.

Nostril

Snout of an epaulette shark

NICE NOSE
Water is taken in through the epaulette's big nostrils and passed to a nasal sac where odors are smelled. Sharks can detect very weak odors – as little as one drop of fish extract diluted over a million times.

SPOTTY NOSE
The spots in front of the nostrils on this sand tiger's snout are sensory pores called ampullae of Lorenzini. The deep pores are full of jelly and connect at their base to nerves; they detect weak electrical signals produced by a prey's muscles and bodily processes. Sometimes sharks are confused by electrical signals given off by metal, so they will bite shark cages (pp. 52–53).

Reproduction and laying eggs

FOR SOME SHARKS, finding a mate means a long swim, because males and females often live in different parts of the ocean. When they meet, the male chases the female, biting her to encourage her to mate. He inserts one of his claspers (extensions of his pelvic fin) into her cloaca, or body opening (pp. 10–11). Seawater already drawn into a sac in the male's body is then squirted into a groove in his clasper. This water flushes sperm into her cloaca. In this way, the sperm fertilizes the female's eggs inside her body. In contrast, in bony fish, fertilization occurs outside the body, with sperm and eggs being shed into the water. Some female sharks can store sperm until they are ready to reproduce, so fertilization may not happen immediately. Most sharks give birth to live young (pp. 22–23), but some reproduce by laying eggs. The fertilized eggs are encased in a leathery shell and deposited by the female on the seabed, where the embryos, or developing shark pups, grow until they are ready to hatch. These sharks are oviparous, which means their young hatch from an egg laid outside the mother – just like birds and bony fish.

MERMAIDS
Mermaids are mythical sea creatures with a woman's body and a fish's tail. Since ancient times, sailors have made up stories about mermaids. The empty egg cases of dogfish and rays that wash up on the seashore are called mermaids' purses.

SPIRAL EGG
A horn shark wedges its spiral-shaped egg case into rocks, protecting it from predators.

CAT'S EGG
The cat shark's egg case is firmly anchored onto anything growing on the seabed. Shark eggs are large and well protected; because of this they stand a better chance of survival than the masses of small eggs laid by bony fish.

CATCH ME IF YOU CAN
This male whitetip reef shark is pursuing a female in the hope that she will mate with him. He may be attracted by her smell.

LOVE BITES
When a male whitetip reef shark gets close to a female (right), he bites her to arouse her interest. He will also grab her pectoral fin in his jaws to keep her close to him during mating. Very little is known of the mating habits of other large sharks.

THICK SKIN
Some female sharks, like this blue shark, have much thicker skin than males, which prevents serious injury during courtship. Most "love bites" are only skin deep and heal in a few weeks.

MATING SHARKS
People rarely see sharks mating in the wild, or even in aquariums. From a few observations, it seems that larger sharks mate side to side. Whitetip reef sharks (left) mate side to side and may pivot on their heads. The male of smaller sharks, such as dogfish (or cat sharks), is more flexible and wraps himself around the female when mating.

DOGFISH EGGS
Every year female small spotted cat sharks, also known as lesser spotted dogfish, lay about 20 eggs in seaweed. The developing dogfish lie safe inside their egg cases. At first the egg cases are soft, but soon they harden in the seawater. The tendrils at the corners of the egg capsules anchor them to seaweed to prevent them being swept away by currents. Embryos take about eight to nine months to develop before they are ready to hatch. During this time each embryo gets its nourishment from its large yolk sac.

Tendril

Dogfish embryo

Yolk sac

Pair of dogfish egg cases

Pair of ten-day-old dogfish

Cream-colored underside

DOGFISH PUPS
These young dogfish are only ten days old. They are only 4 in (10 cm) long, and they look like small versions of their parents. Shark pups are generally much larger and more developed than young of bony fish. Soon after hatching, the young dogfish start to feed on small creatures like shrimp. It will be ten years before they reach maturity and start to breed. When fully grown, dogfish are about 3 ft (1 m) long.

1 ONE-MONTH-OLD SWELL SHARK EMBRYO
Swell sharks live on the eastern side of the Pacific Ocean in shallow coastal waters. They are called swell sharks because when threatened they wedge themselves into a rocky crevice by gulping in mouthfuls of water. If taken out of the water, a swell shark can still swell up by taking in air. The female lays two eggs at a time, depositing them among clumps of seaweed. Each egg is protected by a leathery case. One month after it was laid, the fertilized egg has developed into a tiny embryo. The large egg sac is full of yolk, which nourishes the growing embryo.

Coloring consists of light and dark brown bands, with dark spots on shark's top side

2 EMBRYO AT THREE MONTHS
The embryo has grown much larger and already has eyes and a tail. The yolk sac is connected to the embryo's belly by a cord, and oxygen in the surrounding seawater passes through the leathery egg case so that the embryo is able to breathe.

3 SEVEN-MONTH-OLD EMBRYO
By now the embryo looks much more like a baby shark. It has a complete set of fins and is able to wriggle around inside the egg case. The two rows of spines on the baby's back will help give it a grip on the egg case as it pushes its way out. The baby shark, or pup, will hatch as soon as it has used up the rest of the yolk sac.

4 TWO-MONTH-OLD PUP
After ten months, the young swell shark (6 in, 15 cm long) has hatched from the egg case. This is a most vulnerable moment in its young life because it is so small and there are many predators. Its mottled color pattern makes it hard to see when it is hiding on the seabed. It can also wedge itself into a hiding place by swelling up.

Two-month-old swell shark pup

Live young

THE MAJORITY OF SHARKS give birth to live young instead of laying eggs. Most of these sharks are ovoviviparous: that is, the embryo develops in a large, yolky egg kept inside the female's oviduct, or womblike cavity. The embryos hatch while still inside the mother, develop yet further, and then are born "again" as live baby sharks. In some ovoviviparous sharks, the first pups that develop eat any unfertilized eggs – plus their less developed brothers and sisters – in the mother's oviduct. In sand tiger sharks, for example, only one of the young cannibals survives in each side of the "womb." In viviparous (born live) sharks, such as lemon, blue, and bull sharks, each fertilized egg develops inside a separate compartment in the mother's oviduct. The unborn pup is fed via a placenta. As in humans and other mammals, the placenta acts like a sieve, allowing food and oxygen to pass from mother to baby, and waste materials from baby back to mother, through the connecting umbilical cord.

MOTHER AND BABY
Human babies need to be looked after for many years, but shark pups are not so lucky. They must fend for themselves as soon as they are born.

A LEMON SHARK IS BORN
(1) The tip of the pup's tail is just visible poking out of its mother's opening, or cloaca (pp. 10–11). Pregnant lemon sharks come into shallow coastal lagoons that are sheltered from the waves, to give birth. Scientists studying sharks at Bimini in the Bahamas some- times catch female sharks for their research. (2) Here, the female has begun to give birth. (3) The scientist is acting like a mid- wife, and is helping the passage of the pup out of the mother's birth canal.

HAMMERHEAD PUPS
Hammerhead sharks give birth to live young that are little replicas of their parents. In one litter, up to 40 pups may be born, with their head projections bent back. In the uterus, each pup is connected to its mother by an umbilical cord.

BABY AFRICAN ELEPHANT
A baby elephant takes 22 months to develop inside its mother's womb, which is the longest gestation period of any mammal. The long pregnancy is not surprising, since a baby elephant weighs over 220 lb (100 kg) at birth. Some sharks have a nine-month gestation period, just like humans, though the spiny dogfish matches the elephant in taking 18 to 24 months to be born.

SPINY BABIES GO EASY ON THEIR MOTHERS
Giving birth is hard for any mother. Fortunately for a hedgehog mother, the spines of her babies do not poke out until after birth. The sharp spines on the dorsal fins of newborn spiny dogfish have protective coverings.

BIGEYE THRESHER PUPS
As bigeye thresher pups develop inside the uterus, they feed on bundles of un-fertilized eggs. The pups have long tails – just like their parents.

(4) The lemon shark pup, one of up to 17 pups, is still attached to its mother by the umbilical cord. She is nearly 10 ft (3 m) long, but her pups are only 24 in (60 cm)long.
(5) The pup will rest for a while on the sea-bed, then swim away, breaking the umbilical cord. (6) Now the pup faces life on its own. It must seek the cover of mangrove roots and hide from predators, such as larger sharks and barracudas. For many years it will stay in a small nursery area in the shallows of the lagoon, near where it was born. Then it will make exploratory trips out of the lagoon to the coral reefs and will gradually spend more time farther out to sea.

4

6

5

Teeth and diet

SHARKS CONTINUALLY lose their teeth. When the front ones wear out, they are replaced by new ones growing in another row behind them. An individual shark goes through thousands of teeth in a lifetime. Most animals, like elephants and seals, cannot replace their teeth, and die when the teeth wear out. As the shark grows, its new teeth are larger than the ones they replace. Sharks' teeth come in many shapes according to what kind of food they eat. Teeth like small spikes are used for gripping small prey. Serrated teeth are used for cutting. Long, curved teeth can hold slippery fish. Blunt teeth crunch up shellfish. A few species of shark, like basking and whale sharks, have tiny teeth compared to their great size. They do not use their teeth to feed; they filter food out of the water instead. Some sharks produce different shaped teeth as they grow older.

Tiny teeth of basking shark

Gill rakers

MOUTH WIDE OPEN
Basking sharks swim along with their mouths open to catch shrimp and other small creatures called plankton that drift in the sea. The food is trapped on rows of bristles called gill rakers as the water flows through the mouth and out through the gill slits. The gill rakers are shed each year during the winter months when there is little food around. A new set of rakers grows in the spring, and then the basking sharks can start to feed again.

EPAULETTE EATING
Epaulette sharks live on coral reefs in the southwest Pacific Ocean around Australia and Papua New Guinea. They grow to about 3.3 ft (1 m) long and can crawl along the bottom using their pectoral fins. These sharks search among the shallows and tidepools for small fish, crabs, shrimps, and other small creatures to eat.

Epaulette eating

SMILE PLEASE
Swell sharks (top right) from the eastern Pacific Ocean have big mouths for their 3.3-ft (1-m) length. Armed with rows of tiny teeth, these sharks eat bony fish that rest on the seabed. Only the Port Jackson's rows of small front teeth (bottom right) are visible when its mouth is open. At the back of its jaws are strong, flat teeth for crushing shelled prey.

Mouth of swell shark

CRUNCHY DIET
Port Jackson sharks have small, pointed front teeth to grab their prey. The strong, flat back teeth crunch hard-shelled crabs, mussels (right), and sea urchins (below right).

Section through a Port Jackson's jaws

Mouth of Port Jackson

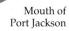

TIGER MOUTH

Tiger sharks cruise the warm waters of the world around islands and coasts of continents and often move in-shore at night to feed.

ALL THE BETTER TO EAT WITH

Tiger sharks have multi-purpose teeth. The pointed tip impales prey, and the serrated bottom edges are for cutting. The teeth are strong and can crunch through a turtle's bones and shell. If a tooth breaks, it is replaced by one growing forward from the row behind.

DAILY MENU

Tiger sharks eat all kinds of food from squishy jellyfish to tough-shelled turtles. They are not put off by the jellyfish's stings or even by venom from sea snakes. Even sea birds are not safe as tiger sharks will grab them from the surface of the sea. Carcasses of land animals washed into the sea, such as chickens, dogs, horses, and cows, are also eaten. Even tin cans, coal, and plastic bags have been found in tiger sharks' stomachs, and occasionally they will attack people.

Sea turtle

Jellyfish

JAWS

A tiger shark's jaws are only loosely connected by ligaments and muscles to the rest of its skull, so it can push its jaws out to take a big bite. When it feeds on large prey, it shakes its head back and forth to tear off chunks.

DISH OF THE DAY

Sand tigers eat a variety of bony fish (left), as well as lobsters, small sharks, and rays.

Goatfish

Lobster

RAGGED-TOOTH SHARK

Sand tigers, called ragged-tooth sharks in South Africa and gray nurse sharks in Australia, reach 10 ft (3 m) in length. Their long, curved teeth get progressively smaller from the front to the sides of the jaw and are ideal for snaring fish or squid. They look fierce but will attack only if provoked.

Friend or foe?

CLAWS
This 0.75-in-long (19-mm) copepod digs its sharp claws into a basking shark's skin. It feeds on skin secretions and blood. Basking sharks, infested by these and other parasites, become irritated. Reports tell of sharks leaping clear of the water to get rid of them.

Claw
Antenna
Head
Thoracic plate, or body section
Abdomen

BARNACLES ABOARD
This strange-looking lump is a barnacle, related to the ones found on the seashore. In the sea, the larvae, or young, of this barnacle attach themselves to dorsal fins of spurdogs or dogfish. The root, or stalk, of this 1-in-long (26-mm) barnacle has rootlets that absorb nutrients from the shark.

Soft shell
Root
Rootlet for absorbing food from shark

LIKE MOST ANIMALS, sharks have a variety of small friends and enemies that choose to live on, in, or near them. Small fish called remoras often hitch rides on sharks using suckers on their heads. Remoras help sharks stay healthy by eating the tiny shellfish called copepods that often infest sharks' fins and gills. Sometimes remoras hitch rides on the bow waves produced by a shark swimming though the water. Other kinds of fish, called pilot fish, also swim with sharks and ride their bow waves. Pilot fish probably feed off scraps left over after a shark's meal. Copepods, tapeworms, and other parasites live on or within sharks, feeding off their skin, blood, or digested food. Parasites may cause a shark discomfort, but they will rarely kill it.

CLEAN TEETH
Other animals have friends too. A bird cleans a crocodile's teeth and finds something tasty to eat.

Female

Male

CLING ONS
These small (0.5 in, 13 mm) crustaceans, or copepods, have adhesive pads to stick onto sharks' fins. They feed on skin secretions.

STREAMERS
Copepods are clinging onto the dorsal fins of this mako shark (above) and have egg cases streaming out behind them. Each case contains a stack of disk-shaped eggs. When the eggs are released, they hatch into tiny young, or larvae. These larvae drift about in the sea, passing through several stages of development before attaching themselves to a passing shark.

STICKING TOGETHER
Shark suckers, or remoras (left), live in the world's tropical oceans. Each has a ridged sucker on the top of its head that it uses to attach itself to sharks and rays. While hitching a ride, remoras often do their hosts a favor by nibbling off skin parasites. They may also steal scraps when the shark has a meal and even feed on the placenta (pp. 40–41), when a shark gives birth to pups (above).

MOBILE HOME
Whale sharks (top) are so big that they provide living space for large numbers of remoras. Some remoras congregate around the mouth, even swimming inside the mouth cavity and gills, where they may feed on parasites; others nestle around the cloaca on a female shark (above). Remoras get free transportation from their giant hosts, by either attaching themselves or riding the shark's bow wave.

WORMS AND MORE WORMS
Hundreds of 1-ft (30-cm) tapeworms may live in a shark's gut, where they absorb food. Segments full of eggs from their tail ends are passed into the sea; the eggs hatch when eaten by a copepod. The young worm is passed to a bony fish when the fish eats the copepod. If a shark eats the fish, the cycle begins again.

Anchor which embeds in eye's surface

Arm

Head

Trunk

Egg sac, containing thousands of eggs

Tentacle

Head

Body

EYE SPY
This strange copepod hangs by its long arms to a Greenland shark's eye. At 1.2 in long (31 mm), the parasite makes it hard for a 20-ft (6-m) shark to see. It feeds on the eye's surface tissues, but once there, it cannot let go.

PILOT FISH
Young golden trevally from the Pacific Ocean swim with larger fish, including sharks. Though they are called pilot fish, they do not guide sharks and other large fish to sources of food. They just like to school with larger fish. They may also be protected from other fish that do not like to be close to sharks. Pilot fish are much too agile to be eaten themselves.

NAVIGATING
A large ship is guided into harbor by pilot boats, but sharks navigate on their own (pp. 18–19).

The great white shark

A POWERFUL PREDATOR, the great white inspires fear. This awesome shark grows to over 20 ft (6 m) long and weighs more than 2.4 tons (2.2 tonnes). It is the largest of the predatory sharks, capable of eating seals whole. The great white became famous in the *Jaws* movies, where it appears as a bloodthirsty creature intent on killing people. Attacks (pp. 48–49) on people are rare and possibly occur when a shark mistakes a person for its usual prey, the seal. Despite its fame, little is known about the great white. Scientists have yet to discover where mating and birth occur, or what the shark's age is when it reproduces or dies. No one knows how many great whites there are, but in some areas they may be on the decline.

FRENCH LANDING
This old engraving of a great white landed on France's Mediterranean coast shows how a century ago people were also fascinated by sharks. Unless they were lucky enough to see sharks firsthand, artists had to rely on descriptions to make their drawings, since there were no photographs. There are several inaccuracies in this engraving – the artist has given the great white gill covers, like bony fish, as well as gill slits, and the tail of a thresher.

Dorsal fin

Small second dorsal fin

Pelvic fin

Long snout

Front view of model of a great white shark

Swimming keel

Upper and lower lobes of caudal fin are almost symmetrical (pp. 16–17)

Relatively small anal fin

Clasper

WARM BLOOD
Great whites and their relatives – the mako, thresher, and porbeagle – are all warm-blooded, which means that they are able to keep their body temperature higher than the surrounding water. Only mammals, birds, and a few fast fish, like the tuna, are warm-blooded. These sharks have blood vessels in their muscles arranged in a complex network, so that the warm blood leaving the muscles passes heat to the cool blood coming from the gills (pp. 10–11). A high body temperature means that great whites have warm muscles which are able to act fast. This is important for a predator that has to make a high-speed dash to catch its prey. Being warm-blooded may also help the great white to digest its food more quickly. Scientists estimate that after a big meal a great white can last three months before needing another one.

Pore, marking position of ampullae of
Lorenzini – sensory organs for detecting
prey's electric field (pp. 18–19)

Long gill
slit – one
of five

Sharp, serrated
(notched) teeth

WHITE DEATH

A great white's
coloring makes it
difficult to see in the
water, so it is able to
sneak up on its victims.
When seen from below, a
shark's white undersides
blend in with a bright sky's
reflection at the water's surface. This
magnificent shark is sometimes called
"white pointer," referring to its pointed
snout which makes it more streamlined. Great
whites often have scratches and scars on their
snouts, which may be the result of their prey fighting
back. They are also sometimes bitten by larger members
of their own kind that move in to take food away from them.

Pectoral fin

Full-length side view
of model of a male
great white shark

TAKING THE BAIT

Scientists, filmmakers,
and photographers use
chum (a mixture of blood
and rotting fish) and other bait to
attract great whites. Great whites are
among the few sharks that stick their
heads out of the water before, and
sometimes during, attacks on prey.
As the shark takes the bait, its eyes roll
back in their sockets revealing the white
surface of the eyeball. This protects the
more vital front part of the eye from
being scratched, which may happen
if the shark is attacking live prey, such
as a seal armed with claws and teeth.

TAGGING A GREAT WHITE

Dr. John McCosker, an American shark scientist, tags a
great white off the Australian coast (top). Sonic tags have
revealed that a great white can cruise at 1.8 mph (3 kph),
traveling about 120 miles (200 km) in three days (above).

Continued on next page

Distribution of the great white shark

BIG BITE
The great white's upper jaw protrudes forward, and its snout tips upward (right) so it can grab a chunk of meat. This shark may realize that there is no danger of its prey retaliating, because the shark's eyes face forward and are not rolled back.

What a great white eats

Great white sharks live in the cool to warm waters along the coasts of North and South America, north and south Africa, the Mediterranean, Japan, China, Korea, Australia, and New Zealand. They also occur occasionally around some islands in the mid-Pacific and Atlantic oceans. They are often seen near seal colonies, where they prey on both adults and young, but only a few sharks seem to hunt in any one area. When attacking a seal, a great white approaches unseen from below, takes a bite, then moves off for a short while. The prey soon weakens because of loss of blood and shock, and the shark can then finish it off easily. The great white's diet changes as it grows older. Young sharks of about 7–10 ft (2–3 m) long eat mostly fish; older sharks around 13 ft (4 m) long tackle larger prey such as seals and sea lions.

ON THE MENU
Great whites eat a variety of animals including bony fish, other sharks, some seabirds, marine mammals (such as seals and porpoises), and, occasionally, people! Great whites are also scavengers and will eat whale carcasses and other dead animals. Unless a great white is seen feeding, it is hard to know if an animal found in its stomach had already died before it was eaten.

Diver for dinner

Leopard sharks (above) are eaten by young great whites along the Pacific coast of North America

Bony fish, such as cabezon (above), are eaten by young great whites along the Pacific coast of North America

California sea lions (right) are eaten by adult great whites

Scientists have found remains of jackass penguins, from South Africa, with bite marks made by great whites

TOP TIGER
Tigers and great whites are the top predators of land and sea, respectively. When they're adults, no animals prey on them, but they are killed by people. Tigers, like great whites, sometimes eat people.

Young elephant seals (above) are easy prey

Gentle giants

HUMPBACK WHALES
Whale sharks are named after those other ocean giants – the whales – which are not fish but mammals.

WHALE SHARKS are the largest fish in the world, reaching at least 40 ft (12 m) long and weighing 13 tons (13.2 tonnes), about as large as an adult gray whale. These docile sharks are harmless and will allow scuba divers to hitch rides by hanging onto their fins; the only danger is in getting scraped by the shark's rough skin, or accidentally knocked by the huge tail as it swings back and forth. These giant fish cruise at 2 mph (3 kph). They live in tropical and subtropical waters, and they feed by filtering food out of the water. Because they feed near the surface, where there is a good supply of food to support their large bulk, they occasionally run into ships. Scientists believe that whale sharks may either lay enormous 14-in (30-cm) long eggs or give birth to live young, hatched from eggs inside their bodies.

NOT MUCH OF A BITE
Whale sharks do not bite or chew food, so they do not need their teeth, which are no bigger than a match head.

Distribution of whale sharks

AT THE DENTIST
People use their teeth to chew food. If their teeth are removed, they need to replace them with false ones.

A GREAT GULP
Despite their huge size, whale sharks feed on plankton (tiny animals that drift in the sea), small fish, and squid. Other large fish, such as basking sharks (pp. 34–35), manta rays (pp. 8–9), and baleen whales, also feed by filtering food out of the water. Whale sharks scoop up water into their huge mouths, and as water passes over their gills and out through their gill slits, food is captured in filters attached to the gills. These filters are made up of a mesh of tissues supported by cartilaginous rods. Whale sharks occasionally eat larger fish such as mackerel and tuna, which are swallowed as they scoop up schools of smaller fish. They can feed in a vertical position, even sticking their heads out of the water and sinking down to draw large fish into their mouths.

White-spotted
bamboo sharks
grow to about
37 in (95 cm) long

Anal fin

Brown-banded bamboo
sharks grow to just
over 3.3 ft (1 m)
long

Nurse sharks grow
to 10 ft (3 m)
long

Barbel

Epaulette sharks grow to just over 3.3 ft (1 m)
long

ONE BIG HAPPY FAMILY
Although they are much smaller, these four
sharks (white-spotted and brown-banded
bamboos, nurse, and epaulette) all belong
to the same group as the whale shark. The
main features they have in common are the
presence of an anal fin and the position of
their mouths well in front of their eyes.
They also have two barbels on the tips of
their snouts that help them find food.
Unlike the whale shark, these much
smaller sharks all live on the seabed.

Basking beauties

WITH THEIR HUGE MOUTHS wide open, basking sharks cruise the ocean like giant mobile sieves, filtering countless tiny creatures from the water. This shark is the second largest fish in the world, after the whale shark (pp. 32–33); it grows to about 33 ft (10 m) long and weighs over 3.6 tons (4 tonnes). Basking sharks often swim at the surface on sunny days with their dorsal fins, and perhaps their snouts or tails out of the water. They are probably more attracted by the concentration of food at the surface than by the sunshine. Unfortunately, when the sharks are at the surface, they make easy targets for fishermen who harpoon them for the oil in their large livers, which may be a quarter of their body weight. These sharks are also killed because of the damage they do to salmon nets. Naturalists are concerned that too many are being killed; little is yet known about these fish – how they reproduce, how they migrate, and how many are left in the wild.

SHARK FISHING
At Achill Island off Ireland's northwest coast, basking sharks were once netted in a bay, then speared with a lance, and dragged ashore. Fishing stopped when the numbers of sharks coming into the bay declined.

Eye

Nostril

Gill arch – water passes through the arch and then through a sieve of gill rakers before flowing over the gills and out through the gill slits

OILY MOUTHS
Oil from sharks' livers has been used in cosmetics like lipsticks.

Nostril

Eye

Gill rakers

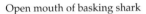

Open mouth of basking shark

OPENMOUTHED
As the basking shark swims along, 400,000 gallons (1.5 million liters) of water flow through its huge mouth each hour. Drifting in the water are tiny creatures like baby crabs, fish eggs, copepods, and arrowworms – all known as plankton – which are strained out of the water by hundreds of long bristles, or gill rakers (pp. 24–25), and trapped in a layer of slime. After a minute the basking shark closes its mouth, emptying the water out through its gill slits before swallowing its food. In winter, when plankton becomes scarce in the cool waters where basking sharks live, they stop feeding and shed their gill rakers. No one knows where basking sharks go in winter, but they may sink to the bottom to rest on the seabed. In spring, basking sharks appear on the water's surface and start to feed again, having grown a new set of gill rakers.

Distribution of basking sharks

SHARKS AT WAR
In World War II some fighter planes used shark oil to lubricate their instruments. These American planes are decorated with shark jaws to frighten the enemy, but the painted sharks have much bigger teeth than basking sharks do.

Angel sharks

IMAGINE RUNNING A STEAMROLLER over a normal-shaped shark – the result would look very much like an angel shark. These strange, flat sharks have extra-large pectoral fins, which resemble angels' wings. Angel sharks spend much of their lives resting on the seabed or lying in wait for fish or shellfish to move within reach of their snapping, sharp-toothed jaws. They can also swim, using their tails to propel themselves along, just as other kinds of shark do. Angel sharks are most active between dusk and dawn, traveling as far as 5.5 miles (9 km) during the night. There are 13 species of angel shark that live in shallow coastal waters around the world and to depths of over 3,300 ft (1,000 km).

MONK FISH
Ever since the 16th century, angel sharks have been called "monk fish," because the shape of their head looks like the hood on a monk's cloak.

The caudal fin, or lower lobe of the tail, is longer than the upper lobe – a feature unique to angel sharks

Second dorsal fin

0   1200   2400   3600   miles

Distribution of angel sharks

Pelvic fin

First dorsal fin

Gill slit

Mouth

Eye

Spiracle

Pelvic fin

Underside of ray

LOOKALIKES
Rays (pp. 8–9) are flat, just like angel sharks. But unlike angel sharks' pectoral fins, a ray's are completely attached to its head, and its gill slits are located on the underside of its body.

Pectoral fin

Top side of ray

ANGELS
This angel shark grows to nearly 6.5 ft (2 m) long. It is found in the Mediterranean and Baltic seas, the eastern Atlantic Ocean, and the English Channel, down to depths of about 490 ft (150 m). Like all angel sharks, it has eyes on the top of its head so it can see while lying flat on the seabed. For respiration (breathing), it draws in water through its large spiracles, which are also on the top of its head. Water taken in through the spiracles is more likely to be free of silt, which could clog up its gills, than water taken in through its mouth.

36

Eye

Spiracle

Pectoral fin

Top side
of angel shark

HEAD START
The head of an
angel shark is
separated from
its pectoral fins.
The gill slits extend
from the side of its
head to under its throat.

Mouth at front of head

Side view of
an angel shark

37

Continued on next page

Japanese wobbegong

Lobe

Barbel

**WOBBEGONG
OF THE ORIENT**
The Japanese
wobbegong lives along the
coasts of Japan, China,
Vietnam, the Philippines,
and Korea, in the western
Pacific. It grows to about
3.3 ft (1 m) in length.
Wobbegongs are not
usually aggressive,
but people have
been bitten when they have stepped
on a hidden wobbegong by mistake.
Fishermen have also been bitten by
wobbegongs caught in their nets.

Undercover sharks

Sharks living on the seabed often have
colors and patterns on their skin. These
sharks, such as wobbegongs and swell
and angel sharks, are able to camouflage themselves, or to blend in with
their surroundings. They have
blotches, spots, or stripes that
make them difficult to see on
sand or among rocks, sea-
weeds, and corals on the seabed.
Wobbegongs have elaborate
disguises, with blotchy skin and
lobes on their head that look like bits of
seaweed. Other sharks, like swell
sharks, hide in crevices; angel sharks
cover themselves with sand. Why hide
if you are a shark with sharp teeth?
These undercover sharks often lie in
wait for prey like fish and crabs to
swim near, then snap them up. Also,
hiding helps small sharks avoid
being eaten by larger predators.

**NOW YOU SEE ME,
NOW YOU DON'T**
It is difficult to see
angel sharks lying on
the seabed – they
are flat and their
mottled skin looks
like sand (top left). To
complete their superb
disguise, angel sharks
(pp. 36–37) partially
bury themselves in the
sand by shuffling their
pectoral fins and
flicking the sand over
their backs (center
left). When the shark is
under a layer of sand,
its eyes poke above the
surface (bottom left)
keeping a look out for
prey. When a fish
comes near, the angel
shark lunges
forward, snapping
its jaws shut
around it. If divers
approach, they may
leave their hiding
place and swim off.
Fishermen catch angel
sharks in nets towed
across the seabed.

AUSTRALIAN SHARK WITH A BEARD
The tasseled wobbegong's beard has
many branched lobes around its
mouth. Its prey – fish and shrimp –
may mistake these for seaweed
and end up being eaten.

MUG SHOTS
Like a prisoner's mug shots, this ornate wobbegong looks different from different angles – from above (top left) and from the side (bottom left). The wobbegong's disguise works just as well from any direction. The Aborigines of Australia gave wobbegongs their wonderful name.

If attacked, a swell shark hides in a crevice and gulps down water, swelling up so that it jams itself in and cannot be pried out.

Ornate wobbegong

Barbel

WHERE'S THE TASSELED WOBBEGONG?
Out of all six wobbegong species, this one has the most branched lobes, or tassels, on its head. Its beard extends around the mouth and down its chin.

A LIFE ON THE SEABED
Wobbegongs spend much of the day lurking on the seabed in the shallows and even in rock pools. They are flat, and their eyes and spiracles are on the upper side of their head, like angel sharks. All wobbegongs have an anal fin; angel sharks lack them. The lobes around their mouth are outgrowths of skin. Even the wobbegong's barbels, or whiskers, on its rounded snout look like fronds of seaweed.

Lobe

39

Horn sharks

Practicing the horn
makes perfect

Horn sharks are named for the two spines on their backs next to each dorsal fin, which look like small horns. The sharks in this group are also called bull-heads because they have broad heads with ridges above their eyes. The shape of the head and the presence of an anal fin distinguish horn sharks from spiny dogfish, which also have dorsal spines.

There are eight species of horn shark; most are no longer than 5 ft (1.5 m). They are found in the Pacific and Indian oceans, where they live on the seabed in shallow water. Horn sharks swim with slow beats of their tails and push them-selves along the bottom with their pectoral fins. The Australian Port Jackson sharks can travel long distances, covering over 500 miles (800 km) to visit their breeding sites. Because horn sharks are slow, scuba divers sometimes tease them by pulling their tails. But they've been known to bite back. Sadly, horn sharks are killed for their spines, which are used to make jewelry (pp. 60–61).

Pelvic fin

A pair of swimming Port Jackson sharks, which are named after an inlet in Australia

Caudal fin

HEAP OF HORNS
Port Jackson sharks often gather in the same area on the seabed, where they rest in groups during the day. Favorite rest sites are the sandy floors of caves or channels between rocks, which may offer some protection against currents. As many as 16 sharks may share the same resting place. At night they become active searching for food such as sea urchins and sea stars.

Spine in front of first dorsal fin

Spine of second dorsal fin

Typical spotted pattern on skin

Eye

Side view of horn shark

Pelvic fin

Gill slit

Eye

Pectoral fin

PIGHEADED
The blunt heads
and big nostrils of
the horn sharks do
look like those of a
pig, which is why
the Port Jackson
sharks are some-
times called
pigfish. They are also called bulldog sharks because
their flat faces and squashed-up snouts make them look
like bulldogs. Yet another name for Port Jackson sharks
is oystercatchers, because they like to eat oysters by
crunching them up with their strong back teeth.

Nostril

*Spine on first
dorsal fin*

*Spine on second dorsal fin – Port
Jackson sharks are killed for their
spines, which are used to make
jewelry (pp. 60–61)*

Anal fin

*Broad, dark
stripe on skin,
typical of Port
Jackson shark*

Pelvic fin

Front view of
Port Jackson
shark

Nostril

Caudal fin

HORN SHARKS
The horn shark from the
coast of California is mainly
active during the night; it
spends the day hiding in
crevices. In some places, its
favorite food is the purple sea urchin.
The purple pigment, or color, is not
broken down when the shark digests
its food. Instead, the pigment stains
the shark's teeth and spines purple.

ALL THE BETTER TO SMELL WITH
Horn sharks, like this Port Jackson,
have very well-developed nostrils. A
good sense of smell may help these
sharks find food, like sea urchins
and shellfish. When the Port
Jackson finds food, it grabs
hold with its sharp front
teeth. The back teeth
(pp. 24–25) are blunt,
for crushing the
shells of its prey.

Head like a hammer

OF ALL THE SHARKS, hammerheads have the strangest-shaped heads. There are nine species of hammerhead, including the bonnetheads, which have only small head projections. The winghead shark has by far the widest head; its head can be half as long as its body. Most hammerheads live in warm temperate and tropical coastal waters. The scalloped hammerhead is one of the most common species and is found in warm waters throughout the world. Large schools of scalloped hammerheads often congregate in areas where there are features on the sea floor like undersea peaks, or sea mounts. A hundred of these sharks may form a school, all of them swimming in unison. At dusk they swim off on their own to feed, and then at dawn they regroup in the same place.

Distribution of hammerheads

Bonnetheads
Wingheads

0   1200 2400 3600
miles

HAMMERHEAD SCHOOLS
There are more females in schools than males, but the reason why they group together is unclear. These large predators have few enemies, so it's not likely that they school for protection. The females compete with each other (often butting one another) to stay in the center of the schools. This may give them a better chance to be courted by the males.

DIFFICULT DIET
Stingrays are the favorite food of the great hammerhead even though the rays are armed with one or more venomous spines, or "stingers," on their tails. Hammerheads do not seem to mind being stung – one individual had nearly a hundred spines sticking into its mouth and gullet.

TWO DIFFERENT SHARKS
The shape of the hammerhead's head (top) compared to that of other sharks – like the tope (bottom) – fascinated early naturalists.

A FINE BONNET
Bonnetheads are the smallest of the hammerheads, reaching only 5 ft (1.5 m) long. The great hammerhead can grow as long as 19.5 ft (6 m). They usually swim together in small groups, but sometimes huge schools of hundreds of sharks congregate near the surface.

First dorsal fin

Gill slit

Mouth

Pectoral fin

Bonnethead shark

Anal fin

Pelvic fin

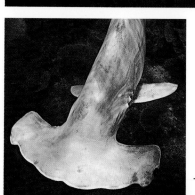

WHY A HAMMER?
No one knows why a hammerhead has a hammer-shaped head, but the broad, flat head may give extra lift to the front of the shark's body as it swims. These two hammerheads (right) differ slightly in that the scalloped one (left) has an indentation in the middle of its head, while the smooth, or common, one does not.

HEAD ON
Hammerheads swing their heads from side to side as they swim along, which gives them an exellent all-around view, since their eyes are right at the tips of their hammers. Their broad heads bear many ampullae of Lorenzini, which sense tiny electric currents generated by their prey.

Scalloped hammerhead

Weird and wonderful

ONE OF THE WORLD'S most extraordinary sharks, the megamouth, was only discovered in 1976. No one had come across this large shark before, though it is over 16 ft (5 m) long and weighs 1,500 lb (680 kg). Since 1976 five more megamouths have been found, including one that was captured alive off the coast of California in 1990. Scientists attached radio tags to this living megamouth so they could follow it (pp. 54–55). The shark spent the day at 450–500 ft (135-150 m) down, feeding on krill (shrimplike creatures). After sunset it ascended to within 40 ft (12 m) of the surface, following its food source, before its descent into the depths at dawn. Another strange shark, the goblin shark, was found nearly 100 years ago, yet scientists know little about it. Other mysteries have been solved. No one knew what caused disk-shaped bites on seals, whales, and dolphins, but the culprits were found to be cookiecutter sharks. Who knows what other weird and wonderful sharks are still to be found deep in the ocean?

Places where megamouths have been discovered

BIG MOUTH
Megamouth means "big mouth," a good name for a shark with a 3-ft (1-m) grin. This shark may lure krill into its huge mouth with luminous organs around its lips. The first megamouth was brought up dead from 660 ft (200 m), entangled in the sea anchor of a U.S. Navy boat off Hawaii. The second was caught in gill nets (long nets in which fish are trapped) off California; the third was washed up and died on a beach near Perth, Australia; a fourth was found dead and a fifth alive off the coast of Japan. The sixth was caught and released off the California coast.

Long snout with sensory pores for detecting prey

Goblin shark

Top side of goblin shark's head

Underside of goblin shark's head

REALLY WEIRD
These ugly sharks (above) were first discovered by scientists off the coast of Japan in 1898. They have flabby bodies and are over 10 ft (3 m) long. Not much is known about these rare sharks that live in deep water at least 530 ft (160 m) down.

GLOWS IN THE DARK
This is one of the lantern sharks, which live in the oceans' dark depths. They are called lantern sharks because they are luminous, or glow in the dark. They are probably the world's smallest sharks, growing to only 8 in (20 cm) long.

Distribution of cookiecutters

BITE SIZED

Cookiecutters have large teeth for sharks only 1.7 ft (0.5 m) long. The common cookiecutter (one of two species) uses its teeth to cut out chunks of flesh from large fish as well as whales, seals, and dolphins. It may wait for such large animals to approach it rather than chasing after them. The cookie-cutter forms a suction cup with its lips, bites, then swivels around to take an oval-shaped plug of flesh. Cookiecutters have also taken bites out of the rubber components of submarines and undersea cables.

GODDESS OF LIGHT

The cookiecutters' scientific genus name, *Isistius*, is from Isis, the Egyptian goddess of light. Cookie-cutters have many light organs on their bellies and glow in the dark. This may attract prey like whales to come close enough to be bitten.

BORING BITES

The wounds on this seal were made by a cookiecutter shark biting into its flesh.

Shark artifacts

MONKEY BUSINESS
This monkey head was made of precious stones by the Aztecs in Mexico. Its teeth are those of a shark.

FOR CENTURIES, people around the world have caught sharks and taken their teeth and skin to make a wide variety of objects, or artifacts. Shark teeth are so sharp that early people were able to make tools and weapons from them. Sharkskin is so hard-wearing that it could be used to make shoes, as well as grips or sheaths for swords and daggers (pp. 60–61). Early people who caught sharks had great respect for these magnificent predators. Fishing for sharks with primitive tools was difficult and dangerous, and stories and legends about sharks were common among seafaring and island people. Sharks were even regarded as gods and were worshipped on some islands in the Pacific. In comparison, early Europeans have few myths about sharks, but sharks do appear in their early natural history books (pp. 28–29).

Large, serrated tooth, probably from a great white shark (pp. 28–31)

CROWN JEWEL
The ten shark teeth that went into making this decorative necklace probably came from great white sharks caught off the coast of New Zealand, where the native Maori live. Today's shark-tooth jewelry, made specially for tourists, contributes to the abuse, rather than the use, of sharks (pp. 60–61).

Pair of fisherman's shoes, made of sharkskin, from India

Sharkskin

Shark-shaped gold weight from Ghana in West Africa

Tin toy, in the form of a shark, from Malaysia

Shark tooth

Shark tooth

Tool, tipped with a shark's tooth, for tattooing people's skin, from Kiribati (the Gilbert Islands), in the western Pacific Ocean

Carved wooden drum, with sharkskin-covered top, 18th century, from the Hawaiian islands in the Pacific

Wooden rasp, covered in sharkskin, from the island of Santa Cruz in the south-west Pacific (below)

Shark skin

Sharkskin-covered grater (below) from the Wallis Islands in the Pacific

Wood knife (right), with cutting edge made of sharks' teeth, from Greenland

Shark skin

SHARKS IN THE HOME
From ancient times, the skin and teeth of sharks have been used to make a variety of household items. Some sharkskin is so rough that it has been used for grating food (left), but if the denticles are removed the soft skin is used like leather for making shoes and belts, or even drums (above). Shark teeth have been used for knives, jewelry, and tools. Other items were made in the shape of a shark because people admired sharks, but toy sharks were made just for fun, as they are today.

FISHING AND WORSHIP

Early people often risked their lives trying to catch sharks from small boats with primitive harpoons. Such heroic deeds often became a test of manhood. In some South Pacific islands, boys would go out in canoes to catch sharks for the island kings. They used rattles (right) to make noises in the water to attract sharks to their canoes. Then the sharks would be lured into a noose and killed with a club. The Hawaiian islanders fished for sharks and used both nooses and lines with hooks (below). They also believed that their dead relatives came back to life in the form of animals, such as sharks. These shark spirits would protect them while fishing. On other Pacific islands, sharks were thought of as gods and were never eaten.

Long spear for catching sharks, from the Nicobar Islands, India

Coconut-shell rattle for attracting sharks, from near Samoa in the South Pacific

Small harpoon for catching sharks, Gambia, West Africa

Shark-tooth necklace from New Zealand

Two hooks for catching sharks: the one from Hawaii (right) is made of ivory; the other (left) is carved in wood and is from the Cook Islands in the southwest Pacific

Solomon Islanders believed a shark-shaped charm would keep large sharks out of their fishing nets (below)

Sea spirit, with a sharklike head, from the Solomon Islands in the southwest Pacific

Early 20th-century rattle, for attracting sharks, from Papua New Guinea, an island north of Australia

Turn upside down to find a dolphin

BARK PAINTING

The Australian Aborigines painted designs on pieces of bark cut from trees. In their paintings, they often reveal what is inside an animal. In this 20th-century bark painting (left), the painter shows the shark's liver, which has two large lobes.

SHARK WEAPONS

Sharp shark teeth were used by people from the Pacific islands as weapons for cutting and slashing their opponents. They made "brass" knuckles and gloves (right) as well as swords, using rows of shark teeth as a cutting edge, instead of metal. Sharkskin was used in other parts of the world, such as Africa and the Middle East, to make scabbards for protecting metal swords (below).

Shark tooth

Shark tooth

Early Hawaiians packed a punch with these "brass" knuckles made of shark tooth

A warrior from Kiribati in the Pacific would put his fingers into the loops of this glove, to cover his forearm with rows of teeth

Sword used by the Ashanti people of Ghana in West Africa

Sharkskin-covered scabbard, or sheath

Gold-plated handle

47

Shark attack

ATTACK AT SEA
Prisoners escaping from Devil's Island off Guyana are attacked by sharks.

Most sharks are not dangerous and will leave people alone. Each year 50 to 75 people are reported attacked by sharks, but only 5 to 10 of these attacks result in death. People are more likely to die in car accidents or drown in the ocean than be killed by a shark. Attacks may occur when a shark mistakes a person for usual prey – a person's foot may look like a fish. A shark may attack if it feels threatened or is provoked. It is dangerous to be in water where there may be sharks, if for example, the water is murky, you have cut yourself, or bait has been put out for fish. Pay attention to local authorities – never swim alone or at night.

WOUNDED SEAL
Elephant seals are what most great whites on the California coast feast on. These sharks usually approach their prey from behind and then take a bite out of it. They wait until the victim is weakened from loss of blood before finishing it off. Sometimes the seal manages to escape by reaching the beach before the shark attacks again.

FATAL SHARK ATTACK
Most fatal shark attacks occur where people surf, swim, or scuba dive, and where there are large sharks, like the great white, swimming close to shore. Attacks can also occur on people escaping from sinking ships or plane crashes far out at sea. Each year the International Shark Attack File records the numbers of attacks reported.

Each year an average of 92 people die by drowning in the sea off Australia's coast . . .

. . . while around eight people die from scuba diving accidents . . .

. . . and less than one person dies from a shark attack.

WARNING SIGN
To avoid being attacked by sharks, pay attention to signs like this one. Sharks may attack people wading in shallow water.

BULL SHARK
The bull shark is one of the four most dangerous sharks in the world, along with the great white, oceanic whitetip, and tiger sharks. The bull shark lives in the warm oceans of the world. It is one of the few sharks that spends time in fresh water, swimming far up rivers such as South America's Amazon and Africa's Zambezi. It can also enter lakes. At 10 ft (3 m) long, bull sharks are large enough to tackle a person and are not fussy what they eat.

NORTH AMERICA

Boston
New York

San Francisco
San Diego

PACIFIC OCEAN

FLORIDA

HAWAIIAN ISLANDS

SOUTH AMERICA

0   1200   2400   3600 mi

GREAT WHITE SHARK
The *Jaws* movies gave the great white a reputation for being bloodthirsty. Great whites do attack and kill people, but it may be because they mistake them for their natural prey. Surfers are at risk near breeding grounds of elephant seals and sea lions, where great whites like to hunt.

Distribution of
fatal shark attacks

MEDITERRANEAN
SEA

JAPAN

CHINA

RED
SEA

PERSIAN
GULF

INDIA

Dakar

Monrovia

INDIAN
OCEAN

ATLANTIC OCEAN

SOUTH
AFRICA

Mombasa

AUSTRALIA

Durban

Brisbane

East London

Perth

Sydney

Cape Town

Adelaide

Melbourne

SHARK BITE
There have been a number of
attacks on surfers sitting or
lying on their boards.
A shark bit this
board in
two.

TIGER SHARK
Tiger sharks eat almost anything, from turtles,
seals, jellyfish, dolphins, sea birds, sea snakes, to
junk like tin cans. They may be tempted to eat any
animal, including people.

DUMMY ATTACK
Wet suits do not protect against
shark attack, as this experiment with
a dummy shows, nor do colored or
patterned wet suits repel sharks.

SHARK'S-EYE VIEW
Attacks on surfers occur near seal or
sea lion breeding colonies, when
surfers have dangled their arms
or legs over the edge of their surf
boards. Sharks can mistake surfers
for seals because they have similar
shapes when seen from below.

NORMAL SWIMMING
Gray reef sharks live near
coral reefs in the Indian
and Pacific oceans
and grow to about
8 ft (2.5 m) long.
During normal
swimming, the back
is gently curved and
the pectoral fins held
straight out from the body.

THREAT POSTURE
If a diver approaches too close
or surprises a gray reef
shark, it may adopt
this threat posture.
The shark arches
its back and holds
its pectoral fins
downward. It may
also swim around
in a figure eight. If the
diver does not swim slowly
away, the shark may attack.

Sharks at bay

PEOPLE WHO GO into the water where there may be dangerous sharks run a small risk of being attacked. There is no simple way to keep sharks away from all the places where people wade, swim, surf, or scuba dive. Shark-proof enclosures have been built, but these can only protect small areas because of the large cost. In South Africa and Australia, nets are used along the most popular beaches to trap sharks. These nets also trap and kill many harmless sharks, dolphins, rays, and turtles. Tests are being done to see if electric barriers can be used that would keep sharks away without killing them or other animals. Scuba divers occasionally carry bangsticks (tipped with an explosive cartridge), but often an inquisitive shark can be simply pushed away with a long, sturdy stick or club. If all else fails, kicking or punching a shark's snout may discourage them from attacking.

JONAH AND THE ?
In the Bible story, Jonah was swallowed by a large sea creature, which could have been a shark, instead of a whale, as the story claims.

LIFEGUARDS
Australian lifeguards must watch out for sharks. If sharks are spotted near a beach, the shark alarm is sounded and swimmers leave the water. The beach may be closed for the rest of the day, if sharks stay in the area. Always follow a lifeguard's advice on safe swimming.

BLOWN AWAY!
A tiger shark is brought aboard after being killed with a bangstick. The stick fires on contact, tearing apart the shark's insides.

Float
Net
Anchor

IN THE BAG
One way to help people who end up in the sea if a ship sinks or an airplane crashes is to give them large inflatable bags. When the U.S. Navy tested the bags, sharks avoided them, because they could not see any limbs, sense any electric signals, or smell blood or body wastes, which are kept in the bag.

ONE LESS SHARK
A shark, trapped in a mesh net off an Australian beach (right), is landed. During a 17-month period in the 1930s, 1,500 sharks were caught by this method. Since then numbers of sharks have decreased sharply.

Float
Net
Anchor

NETTING BEACHES
Popular beaches are protected by mesh nets that trap sharks. The nets do not form a continuous barrier, so sharks may be caught swimming either toward or away from the beach. Heavy anchors keep the nets on or close to the bottom, and floats keep the top of the net suspended in the water. The nets are about 330 ft (100 m) long and 20 ft (6 m) deep. Marker buoys float at the surface so the nets are easily found again. The nets are checked almost every day and dead sea animals removed. After three weeks the nets need to be replaced because they become fouled by seaweed and other marine growth, and so can easily be seen and avoided by sharks. Nets that have become tangled up in storm waves also need to be replaced.

CHAIN WALL
This wall (left) of interlinked chains surrounding an Australian beach prevents any sharks from getting in. Such walls are too costly to protect more than a couple of miles of beach. Chemical repellents have also been tried, but they are not effective, as any substance released around a person in the water disperses too quickly in the waves.

PROTECTED BEACH
Experiments using screens made of bubbles released from air hoses on the seabed have been tried, but shark nets, as on this Australian beach (above), still seem to offer the best protection.

INVISIBLE BARRIER
Sharks are very sensitive to electric currents, and here an invisible electric barrier is being tested. When the current is off (top) the lemon shark swims past, but when the current is switched on (left) the shark turns back to avoid it. Cables and even portable devices that produce electrical pulses to deter sharks have been tested in the sea.

DEATH NETS
Mesh nets, used to protect beaches, kill many sharks, like the great white (above) and hammerhead (left). Trapped sharks suffocate: when a shark can't swim, it can't keep water flowing over its gills. Up to 1,400 sharks – many of which are harmless – plus many dolphins, are caught each year in South African nets.

SHARK REPELLENT
The American scientist Dr. Eugenie Clark discovered that the Moses sole from the Red Sea produces its own shark repellent. When the sole is attacked, milky, toxic secretions ooze out its skin, so the shark spits it out.

In the cage and out

DIVING SUIT
In the early 19th century, divers wore heavy helmets or hard hats and had air pumped down tubes from the surface. Tall tales were often told about attacks by giant octopuses.

DIVING WITH LARGE predatory sharks can be dangerous, so people who want to get close to sharks, like underwater photographers and filmmakers, use a strong metal cage to protect themselves. No one sensible would want to be in the water with a great white shark (pp. 28–31), unless protected by a cage. For smaller and less dangerous species, like blue sharks (pp. 56–57), divers sometimes wear chainmail suits. The chain mail is sufficiently strong to keep the shark's teeth from penetrating the skin if it should bite, but bruising can still occur. Divers may also have a cage just to retreat into, should the sharks become aggressive. Chum (pp. 28–29) and baits are put in the water to attract sharks, which may become excited by the presence of food and snap at the divers. When sharks are being filmed or photographed from outside a cage, safety divers should also be present to keep watch for sharks approaching from outside the filmmaker's field of vision.

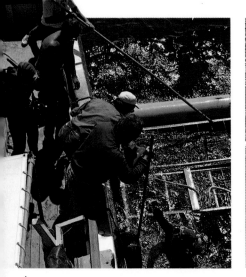

1 LOWERING THE CAGE INTO WATER
Once the dive boat reaches the right place for great whites, chum is thrown into the water, creating an oily slick, and the metal cage is lowered into the sea.

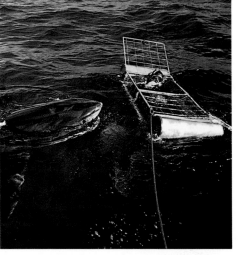

2 A GREAT WHITE APPROACHES
It may be several days before a great white comes close to the cage, kept on the water's surface by floats. The diver can close the lid of the cage for complete protection, if a shark closes in.

3 A VIEW FROM INSIDE THE CAGE
Baits such as horsemeat and tuna attract the shark near the cage. The bars are close enough together to prevent the great white from biting the photographer, but sharks, attracted by metal, may bite the boat and cage.

IN SHINING ARMOR
Famous shark film-maker Valerie Taylor tests the effectiveness of the chain-mail suit. The blue shark (left) is tempted to bite because the sleeve of the suit has been stuffed with pieces of fish. Problems may occur if the shark gets its teeth caught in the chain mail – in its struggle to get free, it could pull Valerie's glove right off. The suits are also heavy, so swimming is difficult. Chain mail was first used by medieval knights to protect themselves from being slashed by swords. Nowadays, butchers also use chain-mail gloves (top) to protect their hands from being cut when they slice meat.

FILMING SHARKS
Australian film-makers Ron and Valerie Taylor are well known for their work on sharks. Ron Taylor films a white-tip reef shark taking a bait (right), while a blue shark approaches the camera (below right).

4 GREAT WHITE SWIMS BY
Divers can be shaken off their feet if a powerful great white should bump into their cage. Such close-up views of the sharks reveal just how big these awesome creatures really are.

Studying sharks

HMS *CHALLENGER*
This British research vessel took 19th-century naturalists to the Atlantic, Pacific, and Indian oceans, where all kinds of marine life including sharks were collected.

Sonic tag

Tagging pole loaded with dart tag

Dart ready for insertion

Return address label

IT IS DIFFICULT to study sharks in the wild, because they constantly move around, swim too fast, and dive too deep for divers to keep up with them. Some sharks, such as hammerheads, are even scared away by bubbles produced by scuba divers. To follow sharks, scientists catch them and attach sonic tags to their fins. When the sharks are released, scientists can keep track of them by picking up radio signals with a receiver. Great care is taken to keep sharks alive when they are caught for tagging and other studies. Also, certain types of sharks are captured and placed in aquariums, where they can be easily observed (pp. 62–63).

Dr. John McCosker tracking sharks in Australia

Propeller measuring a shark's swimming speed is attached to fin of a mako shark

STUDYING LEMONS
Dr. Samuel Gruber has studied lemon sharks in the Bahamas for over 10 years. They do not mind being handled and do not need to swim to breathe, so they can be kept still while scientists make their observations. In this experiment (right), a substance is being injected into the shark to show how fast it grows. Young lemons, too, can have tiny tags inserted in their dorsal fins and are identified later by their own personal code number.

CHECKING UP A SHARK'S NOSE
American scientist Dr. Samuel Gruber checks the flow of water through this nurse shark's nose. Scientists have to be careful because, although nurse sharks are usually docile, they can give a nasty bite (pp. 18–19).

SCIENTISTS' FAVORITE

The lemon shark is one of the easiest sharks to study, both in aquariums and in the sea. A young lemon shark (left) attacks her food. When she eats, she shakes her head vigorously, scattering a large amount of debris in the aquarium's water.

TAGGING TIGERS

Scientists tag a small tiger shark in the Bahamas (top). Sometimes sharks need to be revived after this, so a diver (above) is pushing a large tiger shark along to keep water flowing over its gills.

KEEPING DRY

To go underwater without getting wet, Charles William Beebe (1877–1962) used this bathysphere in 1934 to reach a depth of 3,028 ft (923 m). Sharks as deep as 12,000 ft (3,600 m) are attracted by bait near the surface.

THE FRILL OF IT ALL

Three of these strange sharks (below) were caught off Japan in deep water during the 1870s *Challenger* expedition.

Frill shark

Sixth gill slit – most sharks have only five

Tagging sharks

SOME ANGLERS HELP SCIENTISTS find out where sharks go and how fast they grow by measuring, tagging, and releasing the sharks they catch. Tens of thousands of sharks have been tagged since the 1950s, off the coasts of Australia, the U.S., Africa, and the UK. A few tags are recovered when fishermen catch these sharks again. The record is for a male Australian tope, first tagged in 1951 and recaptured in 1986, 133 miles (214 km) from its original release site. It had grown by 7 in (17 cm). Blue sharks are among the greatest ocean travelers. One tagged near New York was caught 16 months later off Brazil, 3,700 miles (6,000 km) away; another tagged off the British coast was recaptured off Brazil, 4,350 miles (7,000 km) away.

Australian certificate (top) and card (bottom) for details of captured shark

Two Australian applicators with nylon and plastic tags

Tag

Metal tip pierces shark's skin

Where blue sharks have been tagged, released, and recaptured

- Cornwall, UK
- West Africa
- U.S. Eastern Seaboard

0   600   1200   1800 miles

BIRD RINGING
Ringing bands around young birds' legs gives information on migration – just as tags do for sharks – if they are caught again.

Bait

1 **TAGGING/RELEASING SHARKS**
Like most sharks, blue sharks have an excellent sense of smell and are attracted to boats by a dangling chum bag over the side containing smelly, salted fish. The chum's oil spreads out in a thin film over the water's surface, attracting sharks from a great distance. The shark hooks are baited with freshly caught mackerel, and the fishing lines are let out to depths of 40-60 ft (12–18 m).

2 **HOOKED**
Attracted by the oil and blood, the blue shark has taken the bait.

3 **REELING IN**
The shark is reeled in near the boat, very carefully, so as not to damage the shark.

6 TAGGING DORSAL FIN

The tag is made of strong metal that will not corrode in seawater and cause the numbered plastic tag to drop out. On the reverse side of the tag is an address where the tag can be sent, should another angler or fisherman catch the tagged shark again in another part of the world.

Red flag, symbol of British Shark Angling Club

Pale blue flags show two sharks were released

7 RELEASING

Holding the shark by her tail, the skipper gently lowers her back into the sea. Once in the water, the shark swims away as fast as she can.

5 HOLDING THE SHARK DOWN

This female blue shark is 5 ft (1.5 m) long and weighs about 50 lb (22.5 kg). The skipper holds her down and gets ready to insert the tag. The shark can tolerate being out of the water for only a few minutes, so he has to work quickly to put the tag into her dorsal fin. Buckets of salt water are thrown onto the shark to help keep her alive. In other tagging studies, the shark is brought close to the boat but not landed, to avoid damaging it. Then a pole is used to stick the tag into the shark (pp. 28–29).

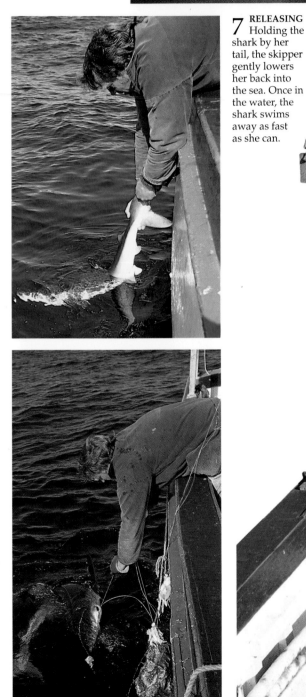

4 THRASHING SHARK

The skipper begins to haul the thrashing shark in, but it fights every bit of the way.

Shark overkill

PEOPLE KILL SHARKS for their meat, fins, skin, and liver oil, as well as for pure sport. Sport fishing can reduce the numbers of sharks found locally, but the biggest threat to sharks is overfishing worldwide. Sharks caught on long lines and in fishing nets are often thrown back into the sea dead, because it is other fish hauled in at the same time that are wanted. Sometimes just the shark's fins are removed and its body thrown back. Sharks are also killed each year in nets to protect swimmers. Sharks have a much slower rate of reproduction than bony fish and take a long time to mature. If too many are killed, their numbers may never recover. Efforts are now being made to protect sharks by creating reserves and restricting how many are caught.

ANGLING
Angling (fishing with a hook and line) is a popular sport. Fast, strong sharks represent a big challenge. Today, angling clubs are becoming more aware of conservation, and some are restricting the size of shark that can be landed. Increasingly, anglers are encouraged to release sharks, instead of killing them (pp. 56–57).

WALLS OF DEATH
Drift nets (top), some 50 ft (15 m) deep and many miles long, are used to catch fish. The nets are so fine that fish do not see them and become trapped in the mesh. Sharks, like this oceanic whitetip shark (above), are easily caught, along with seabirds, turtles, and dolphins.

WHITE DEATH
For many anglers, the great white (above) is the ultimate trophy. People are frightened of great whites and so kill them, but as one of the sea's top predators, these sharks are important in keeping the natural balance in the ocean. The hunting of great whites is banned in South Africa. In Australia, these sharks are also protected.

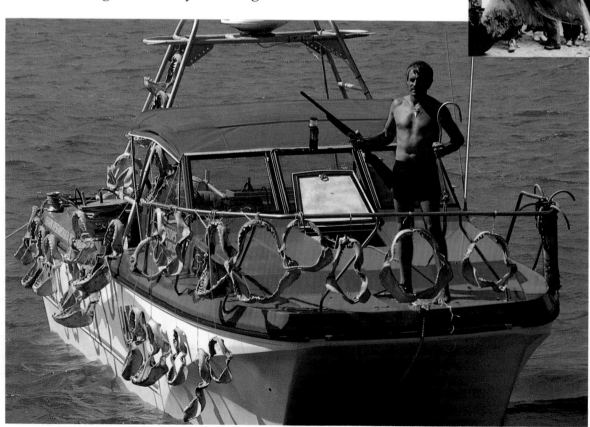

SPORT OR SLAUGHTER
To show just how many sharks were killed, this hunter's boat (left) shows a collection of the victims' jaws.

Drift net

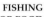

THRASHED THRESHER
Thresher sharks (left) are heavily fished in both the Pacific and Indian oceans. They are caught with long lines and gill nets. Landing a thresher can be dangerous, especially if they lash out with their tails; sometimes their tails get hooked on long lines.

SAD END FOR A TIGER
This tiger shark (right) was killed in an angling competition in Florida. Near some coastal resorts, the numbers of large, predatory sharks – like the great white and tiger – have declined, probably because large numbers of them are still being caught by anglers.

FISHING FOR FOOD
In developing countries, people, like these Asians (left), depend on shark meat for protein. In other countries, shark is often a luxury food in restaurants. Whether we choose to eat shark or not, it is important that shark fishing is controlled. If not, these fascinating creatures could disappear from the world's oceans.

Cutting up sharks for meat

DRYING FINS
Shark fins are used in Chinese cooking for delicacies like shark-fin soup. Because the fins can be dried, they are much easier to market than shark meat, which has to be sold quickly or processed.

Shark fins drying

FINNING
These Japanese fishermen on a boat in the Pacific Ocean are cutting the fins off sharks caught in drift nets. They throw the rest of the shark back in the sea. Fins of many different kinds of sharks are removed, sometimes when the sharks are still alive. When thrown back in the sea, they take a long time to die. Without their fins, they are not able to swim properly and may be torn apart by other sharks.

Use and abuse

PEOPLE HAVE FOUND A USE for almost every part of a shark's body. The tough skin can be turned into leather, the teeth into jewelry, the jaws into souvenirs, the carcass into fertilizer, the fins into soup. The flesh can be eaten, and the oil from the liver may be used in industry, medicines, and cosmetics. Human exploitation of wild animals like sharks can cause a serious decline in their numbers, if more animals are killed than can be replaced by the birth and survival of the young. Sharks are especially at risk because they are slow to reproduce. It is hard to put sensible limits on the numbers of shark that can safely be fished because so little is known about them. Today, sharks are mainly exploited for their meat and fins, and demand for shark meat will probably continue as the human population increases. If fewer people were to use products derived from sharks, their future would be more secure. Otherwise, the effect on the natural balance in the oceans could prove to be disastrous.

NAPOLEON AND THE SHARK
Sailors feared and disliked sharks. Here, the French emperor Napoleon (1769–1821) watches a shark being killed, during his journey into exile on the remote Atlantic island of St. Helena.

SHARK TEETH
These pendants are made from the teeth of the great white shark. Some people mistakenly think that wearing shark tooth pendants make them look as fierce as a great white.

GETTING A GRIP
This sword handle, covered with rough sharkskin, gives a swordsman a secure grip.

In battle, a bloody handle could still be gripped

The sharkskin on the handle of this British Royal Artillery officer's sword has been dyed black

Rough rayskin under black cord

SAMURAI SWORD
This 19th-century sword once belonged to a samurai warrior from Japan. Its handle is covered with unpolished rayskin, and the sheath is made of the polished and lacquered skin of a ray (pp. 8–9).

Carved ivory handle

Lacquered rayskin-covered sheath

PERSIAN DAGGER
The sheath of this 19th-century Persian dagger is covered in rayskin. A flowery design has been painted onto the lacquered skin.

The outside of each door is decorated with "double happiness" characters

BOX OF HAPPINESS
Fine sharkskin, or leather, was used to cover this early 20th-century rectangular box from Korea. The leather is smooth because the denticles, or small teeth, have been highly polished, then lacquered, and dyed dark green. Shagreen – rough, unpolished sharkskin – is used as an abrasive, like sandpaper, for polishing wood.

SHARK REMAINS
These two hammerheads (pp. 42–43) were caught off the coast of the Baja Peninsula in western Mexico. In this poor area, their meat was probably used for food and their skin for making into leather goods, such as wallets and belts.

SHARK AND CHIPS

Much of the fish sold in British fish-and-chip shops is, in fact, spiny dogfish (pp. 22–23), one of the most abundant and heavily fished kinds of shark. Many kinds of shark are given a different name when sold for meat – dogfish is disguised as "rock salmon" in Britain. In the past, people did not like to eat shark because they thought sharks ate the bodies of dead sailors. Sadly, shark steaks are becoming a fashionable delicacy in some restaurants.

JAWS FOR SALE
Many sharks are killed and their jaws sold to tourists as souvenirs. Jaws of large sharks, like the great white (pp. 28–31), fetch high prices. The sale of great white jaws is now banned in South Africa.

HEADLESS CORPSE
This shark was killed for sport and had its head cut off so its jaws could be removed. Shark jaws are popular trophies in the same way that hunters show off the head and horns of deer they have shot.

SHARK LIVER OIL PILLS
In some countries people believe that shark oil can cure all kinds of ills. Shark oil is composed of many different substances, including vitamin A, but this vitamin can now be made artificially.

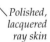

Polished, lacquered ray skin

A cluster of shark liver oil pills

Two bowls and a can of an Asian delicacy – shark-fin soup

SHARK-FIN SOUP
The cartilaginous fibers in shark fins are made into soup, which some Asian cultures regard as a delicacy. The dried fins are soaked and repeatedly boiled to extract the mass of gelatinous fibers. Many other ingredients are then added to these noodle-like fibers to give the soup some taste.

SKIN CARE
Shark oil is used in costly skin creams that are meant to prevent wrinkles and signs of aging. But other creams, based on natural plant oils, are just as effective.

Save the shark!

SHARKS HAVE A BAD reputation as blood-thirsty killers. But only a few kinds of sharks are dangerous (pp. 48–49) and attacks on people are rare. Other animals like tigers and even elephants, which also occasionally kill people, are more popular. Naturalists and other people are concerned because sharks are increasingly threatened by overfishing (pp. 58–59). Some sharks, like lemon sharks in Florida, also suffer because of the destruction of mangrove swamps, which are important nurseries for their pups. Many people begin to like and admire sharks as they learn more about them. In an aquarium, people can observe the grace and beauty of sharks. Good swimmers can learn to snorkel and scuba dive, and may be lucky enough to see sharks in the sea. In some areas, scuba divers are taken on trips to specific places where they can observe sharks in the wild.

MAD ABOUT SHARKS
This crazy sculpture of a blue shark on the roof of a house near Oxford, England, shows just how much some people like sharks.

Making sketches of various sharks in an aquarium

TANKS FOR THE VIEW
Seeing sharks come within inches of your nose is a great thrill, even if there is a glass wall in between (right). But not all kinds of sharks can be kept in aquariums. The fast-moving blue sharks and makos are used to roaming over great distances and need much more space than there is in an aquarium. A great white shark was once kept in an aquarium for a few days, but it became disoriented, continually hitting its nose against the glass, so it had to be released into the sea. Smaller sharks, like smoothhounds (pp. 14–15), are the easiest to keep in an aquarium.

Face to face with a shark (right) and feeding time at the aquarium (far right)

Sand tiger shark

White-tip reef shark

CANDID CAMERA
Taking photographs of sharks in aquariums is a good way to start getting to know them. Photographing moving subjects behind glass is not easy, but perseverance will pay off. Use a film with a fast speed, because aquariums have little light. Ask permission to photograph, but do not use a flash if there are signs prohibiting this. Hold the camera flat against the side of a tank to prevent light bouncing off the glass, if using a flash. Wait for the whole body of the shark to come into view before taking a photograph, but remember that it moves fast!

Cat shark

Photographs taken in an aquarium

LEARNING ABOUT SHARKS
Join a conservation organization that works to help protect marine life in the oceans and seas. Look out for informative articles in wildlife magazines and for other books about sharks. There are also interesting programs on television, which, unlike the scary *Jaws* movies, tell the real story about sharks. Volunteer to help marine biologists in their research, for example, with the Earthwatch program in the Bahamas in the Caribbean. There is still so much more to be discovered about sharks.

A sketch of a classic requiem shark, with its streamlined body and highly efficient system of movement that complements its predatory lifestyle

A typical mackerel shark, which is stouter than a requiem shark

Sketching sharks can be fun as well as useful

SHARKS ON FILE
Visiting aquariums, keeping a shark notebook, drawing pictures of sharks, or copying them from photographs are good ways of seeing how many different kinds of sharks there are. Compare the sharks' colors, variety of skin patterns, and the different body shapes. Eventually, a valuable shark information file can be built up. Write down the size, diet, natural habitat, and the way the various sharks differ. On sketches, label their external features, like fins, gill slits, eyes, and mouth. With some effort, anyone can become knowledgeable about sharks.

Writing down your observations can help build up a valuable shark information file

Pastels

Pencils